VICTORIA OLASEGHA

The Journey's End

FRIENDS THOMAS
PUBLISHING

First published by Friends of Thomas Publishing 2022

Copyright © 2022 by Victoria Olasegha

This novel is entirely a work of fiction. The names, characters and incidents portrayed in it are the work of the author's imagination. Any resemblance to actual persons, living or dead, events or localities is entirely coincidental.

Victoria Olasegha asserts the moral right to be identified as the author of this work.

Second edition

ISBN: 9798678609731

Editing by Ufuomaee

This book was professionally typeset on Reedsy. Find out more at reedsy.com

Contents

Acknowledgement		v
1	Chapter 1	1
2	Chapter 2	8
3	Chapter 3	16
4	Chapter 4	23
5	Chapter 5	31
6	Chapter 6	38
7	Chapter 7	44
8	Chapter 8	56
9	Chapter 9	64
10	Chapter 10	68
11	Chapter 11	77
12	Chapter 12	84
13	Chapter 13	91
14	Chapter 14	101
15	Chapter 15	107
16	Chapter 16	114
17	Chapter 17	121
18	Chapter 18	128
19	Chapter 19	135
20	Chapter 20	141
21	Chapter 21	148
22	Chapter 22	156
The Epilogue		160

Author's Note   163

About the Author   165

Also by Victoria Olasegha   166

Acknowledgement

I am indebted to several people in the writing of this book. I would like to thank my sister, Lois Leke Amoo, and my parents, who have been my greatest cheerleaders since I started writing as a child. I want to also thank my husband, Korede, who earnestly believed in this project and was my greatest encouragement.

I would like to thank my editor, Ufuomaee, and my beta readers, Gloria Briggs and Tara Fagbemi, who gave me invaluable feedback on this project.

1

Chapter 1

Brian let out a whoop. "I can't believe it!"

His eyes widened in amazement. It was what he had always wanted. He circled her, admiring every curve and plane. No doubt about it, she was beautiful. She was his!

He glanced at his father, who stood a few feet away from him. "I can't believe you did this, dad," he breathed.

"It's nothing..." Kevin Anderson shrugged and looked at his son, feeling happier with every passing moment that he had decided to splurge and buy his son this well-deserved gift.

Ever since he was five, Brian had wanted to be a pilot. As far as Kevin was concerned, there was nothing wrong with helping his son achieve his ambition a little faster. "I try to do my best," he said with false modesty.

"When do I get to fly her?" Brian asked breathlessly, rubbing his hands together in anticipation. He could hardly take his eyes off the plane. She was a small plane that could take up to eight passengers. It was the new Cessna Citation Ultra mode complete with the latest electronic gadgets.

Kevin wrinkled his brow as if in deep thought. "I was thi

like...right now?" He grinned, almost chuckling, at the look of awe on Brian's face. Before his son could respond, he beckoned to Brian's flight instructor, who had been waiting behind them as Brian admired his gift.

"Let's do this!" Brian cheered and climbed into the plane with the instructor. He was so glad he had taken those summer flying lessons. He had never dreamed he would be using them so soon. He spent a few minutes learning about the different controls on the dashboard, and after what seemed like forever, they were in the air.

Kevin watched his son zoom around in the sky after a few false starts. The plane nosedived for a moment before zooming upward again. Kevin had no fears regarding Brian's handling of the plane. No doubt about it.

At nineteen, Brian was a man's man; the kind of son that would make other fathers green with envy. He deserved the gift. He was the kind who made all the sports teams, was captain of the football team, yet got straight 'A's in school. He'd made an excellent score on his SATs, which had secured him admission into Yale. He didn't do drugs; he was fearless and intelligent. What more could a father ask for?

His son gave him a carefree wave from the sky, and Kevin waved back with a grin. Brian was certainly a chip off the old block; strong, smart, and independent. Kevin vowed he would do everything he could to keep him that way, even if he had to subscribe to unconventional parenting styles.

*****

Craig inched round the plane in wonder. He has been Brian's best friend since the fifth grade. Their friendship started in an unusual manner. They had a fight, the kind of fight that happens commonly on the playground, where the reason for the fight is obscure, and at the end, despite the bleeding noses and bruised knuckles, there seems to be no victor nor vanquished. Later, they were grateful for the fight, as it ended up making them best friends.

Craig and Brian were very different in terms of personality, academic prowess, and family upbringing. There was also the added issue of race, as Brian was mixed-race, and Craig was black, but they were closer than many brothers. Brian was grateful for that as he felt his mixed parentage made it difficult for him to fit in. Craig never treated him like he was different, and he even felt at home with Craig's family, and vice-versa.

"Man, your dad must have a mighty crush on you or something," Craig said, shaking his head. "She's a beauty. What will you call her?"

"I have no idea yet. Beauty maybe?" Brian responded with a facetious grin.

"I guess you could go anywhere you wanted with this thing. Why don't we take it on a trip to Hawaii?" Craig asked, half-joking.

Brian's face widened in shock. "Are you kidding? My dad wouldn't want me to fly it anyplace that wasn't under his nose."

"Aw, come on. It can't be that hard. Your dad wouldn't have given you such an incredible gift if he didn't want you to have fun with it."

Brian shook his head. "His idea of fun and mine might not necessarily be the same thing."

"It wouldn't hurt to ask, especially now that you've got your license," Craig suggested.

"Maybe. But not Hawaii anyway. If I could go anywhere, I might as well go somewhere exotic."

Craig raised his eyebrows. "Hawaii's not exotic?"

Brian scrunched up his face. "Nah. It's always too crowded."

Craig's face lit up. And then he said in mock seriousness, "I know... How about Timbuktu?"

Brian gave a short laugh. "Nice try."

Craig's phone beeped as a notification came in. It was from Tess, his new girlfriend. She was coming to see him at work, so he needed to be on his way.

He looked up to see Brian watching him. "Hey, man, I've got to get a move on. I, unlike you, have got work to do," he said, squaring his shoulders.

"Yeah," Brian mocked. "It must be a lot of work winking at all those pretty old ladies and chicks that come to the travel agency."

Craig had been working as a ticket salesman at the travel agency all summer. It didn't pay much, but he liked it, and it was an easy way to meet girls. Besides, it beat working in his mother's restaurant, waiting on tables. He had always thought that kind of job was not meant for him.

"What can I say? It's not my fault that I have irresistible charm."

"Hmm. Maybe you could use some of that charm on my father..."

"Hate to disappoint you, kid, but my charm is gender-biased," Craig chuckled, giving Brian a mock salute before sauntering off.

*****

Kevin slowly sipped a cup of coffee while studying his computer screen. He felt satisfied as he looked at the figures in front of him.

His dream of becoming a multimillionaire was going to be achieved faster than he had ever imagined. His lips turned up as he thought about his latest purchase. The airplane, undoubtedly the first of many was so beautiful. Now he could travel with his family in even more style and luxury than just travelling in first class. How far he had come from his impoverished childhood many years ago.

He hadn't always had money or security. He remembered how he had felt as a kid when he and his brother would run and hide whenever they heard their father's footsteps approaching their apartment door. His father was a bully who never let an opportunity to maltreat his wife and children slip by. But it was worse when he was drunk. That was when the blows began.

He and his brother lived in constant fear and dread. Kevin vowed never to grow up to be like his father. He promised himself that if he ever had a son, he would be the best father he could ever be.

Kevin was lucky to have a bright mind and a head for numbers. Those attributes got him a scholarship to Yale, where he obtained a degree in Accounting, and since then, he had never slowed down. Kevin had developed an investment portfolio and had gone into real estate; a decision that had made him millions. He only wished his mother was alive to see how successful he had become.

He had lost his mom in a freak accident while he was in college. His brother had left the country and now lived somewhere in the Middle East, far, far away from the city of his childhood memories. The bully he called his father now lived in a nursing home, sad and alone, just like he deserved, Kevin thought to himself.

A phone call interrupted his reverie.

"Excuse me, Sir," his secretary said apologetically. "There's a Mr. McCarthy here to see you. He doesn't have an appointment, but he said he knew you would be happy to see him."

"McCarthy," Kevin mused. "The name doesn't sound familiar, but send him in."

Within a few seconds, his secretary ushered in a bald, overweight looking man in his early forties, beaming as if he had won the lottery.

"Hi, Kevin. It's been ages since we last saw each other," McCarthy said, boisterously holding out his hand while Kevin gave him a blank stare. "Don't tell me you don't remember me, man. We went to the same high school and played basketball together."

Light slowly dawned on Kevin's face. It was Josh McCarthy, point guard of his high school basketball team. They had been somewhat friendly then but not too close. The whole team had promised to stay in touch; however, that was eons ago.

Kevin stood up to extend a hand to his old friend. "Josh, I'm sorry," he said, motioning for Josh to take a seat. "It is good to see you. You look good."

"Well, you're looking mighty fine yourself," Josh gushed, taking his seat. Kevin sat also, his lips raised in a slight smile. He knew he was 'mighty fine,' but it was still nice to hear.

Though he was impeccably dressed in an Italian suit, the muscles rippling underneath the suit were visible, and his blond hair was only slightly graying at the temples. He had a distinguished air about him.

"You seem to have done very well for yourself. Your office is huge, not at all like the ones I'm used to."

Josh was right; the office was impressive. Its wood panels, with mahogany chairs and tables, and brilliantly lit interior emphasized how expensive and classy the furnishings were.

"Well, you know how it is... Sometimes you get lucky." Kevin wondered briefly what his friend wanted. His eyes grazed his computer screen, which told the time. "So, Josh, how have you been? Your family? Career?"

"Career? You're the one with the career," Josh said, a trace of bitterness in his tone. "Me, I just have a job. I'm a salesman. I sell shoes now."

"Oh," Kevin muttered. Obviously, Josh wanted to get some money off him.

"As for family... Yes, I have a wife. And two teenagers. You know how kids are; they drive you crazy sometimes."

Not mine, Kevin thought dryly and waited for Josh to continue.

"But I didn't come here to talk to you about my problems. I came to invite you to our class's thirtieth reunion. It's on the 2nd of next month, and the whole team's coming down. You have to be there."

Kevin was taken aback, but he managed to say, "Well, thanks for the invitation, Josh, but I'm afraid..."

"Before you say you can't come, Kev, think about all our teammates and how disappointed they would be if you don't show up. We always were one team. Do it for them, Kevin."

Kevin chewed a bit on this and smiled. "I'll see what I can do."

2

Chapter 2

Donna Anderson ran her hand over the rack of clothes and smiled. This was her favorite store. They had everything from cashmere to lace to the softest cotton. Shopping in Aimee's was truly a rewarding experience.

She eyed an evening gown towards the back of the rack. She loved the cut and knew it would fit her slender but petite body well. Purchasing the red evening gown would make her total number of evening gowns fifty-four. Besides, there was a charity benefit coming up soon, and she needed a new dress for the occasion. The red gown drew attention to her brunette hair, and its vivid color accentuated her hazel eyes. Not bad for a girl who grew up in the projects, she said to herself.

Donna knew she was something of a shopaholic, but she couldn't help it. She grew up in a family that lived from hand to mouth. She had experienced the discrimination and lack of opportunities black people faced daily. She considered herself lucky to have lived in a two-parent household. One where her parents tried their best to provide for their children, and eventually, she got a scholarship into one of the Ivy League schools, where she met her husband, Kevin. Unfortunately, her mother died from breast cancer before she got married to Kevin.

Donna now lived in a home where she could never want for anything. And so whenever she saw something she liked, she bought it immediately. She never needed to save to buy anything anymore. It was a bad habit, and she knew she needed to cut down, but then, her husband wasn't complaining.

As the clerk totaled her purchases at the counter, Donna wondered idly why there wasn't such a thing as a Shopaholics' Anonymous in her area. She could probably benefit from it. At the same time, she was rather proud of herself for landing such a rich, wonderful husband and raising a smart, handsome, and responsible son. Not many of her friends could say the same.

Sometimes, it was tough being married to someone from a different race, but Kevin did his best to understand the issues they faced. Her father found it difficult to understand their relationship and was somewhat suspicious of Kevin, but the arrival of his grandson helped thaw the situation a little. It had even healed the relationship between Donna, her father, and his new wife.

However, Donna was the one who had 'the talk' with Brian. She warned him about the complexities of living as a black man in America. Despite his privilege and mixed background, there was a likelihood that he would be treated differently sometimes, both by white and black people. Thankfully, to the best of her knowledge, Brian was yet to have a negative experience associated with his race.

As Donna walked out of the store, holding her purchase, a gray business suit on display in a store across the hall caught her eye. She hesitated, then walked on. Next time, she told herself. Besides, she would be late for her lunch meeting with her friends, and she wanted to be able to tell them how disciplined she had been.

*****

The atmosphere was eerie. It never failed to impress Brian, as he took a walk down Third Avenue, how quiet the area was. Someone had once told him that the richer the neighborhood, the quieter it became. But Brian liked to think that he lived in a more affluent neighborhood than this, though it was not as quiet. It seemed as if the people on the street were afraid to reveal themselves. Everybody hid behind white picket fences and respectable lawns. It was a far cry from Craig's, where there were drug peddlers on every corner.

Hunched, with his hands in his pockets, Brian walked on till he came to an auspicious white bungalow with a red door. He took a deep breath and tried to act casual as he knocked on the door. Someone immediately opened it and pulled him in.

"Brian, are you crazy? My mom would kill me if she saw you here," Rachel exclaimed in her husky voice. Her eyes were blazing, but Brian didn't mind.

As always, the sight of her took his breath away. There was no other word for it. She was luscious. Brunette, tall, and beautiful, with a figure any man could die for.

Rachel and her family were originally from Mexico but had lived in the States for over twenty years. Craig never failed to remind him how lucky he was to have such a gorgeous girl.

"What are you looking at?" Rachel demanded, her breathing raspy. "I'm talking to you!"

Brian sighed and ran a hand through his hair. "I just had to see you. Besides, I knew your mom would be at work. I've missed you."

Rachel let go of his hand. "Just don't ruin things for me now, Brian. If my mom catches me with you, who knows how long I'll be grounded for?"

"Your mom's living in the dark ages, Rachel. What does she want you to be; a nun? You're already sixteen. She should start treating you like an adult."

"Oh, Brian," Rachel said, sighing and tossing her hair. "You can't understand."

"I'm not sure I want to," Brian muttered, sitting down. She gave him a quizzical look. "I don't think I'd ever want to understand such craziness."

Rachel raised a hand. "Let's talk about something else. Why did you risk life and limb to come looking for me?"

"To rescue you from the dragon, of course."

"Brian!"

"That's only part of the reason. You wouldn't believe what happened to me yesterday." He proceeded to tell her about the plane his father had gifted him.

She pretended disinterest and then said with feigned patience, "Brian, I appreciate your telling me about this very special moment in your life, but what in the world has that got to do with me?"

He was not daunted. "Don't you see, babe? We could fly off into the sunset..."

Rachel raised a weary brow. "Brian..."

"No, I mean it. What would you think of spending the rest of your holidays with me, someplace exotic?"

She eyed him, suppressing a huff. "You're dreaming."

Brian sighed. "For now, but who says dreams can't become reality?"

"Not this dream," Rachel replied, shaking her head.

"Have a little faith, Rachel," he persisted and drew her close to him. "Close your eyes and dream with me a little. Can't you just picture us together on the beach, the waves lapping at our feet, the cool sea breeze on our bodies, and some Spanish music playing softly in the background?"

Rachel laughed. "You're a terrible poet. But you do paint a wonderful picture. I almost wish the dream were true."

"Don't lose hope. Besides, I had another dream. I've been dreaming of it for weeks now."

Rachel glanced at him, a smile playing on her lips. "Oh. And what might that dream be?"

"This..." he said, cupping her face and leaning down for a kiss.

*****

Brian sighed as he entered the house. It was great seeing Rachel, and he didn't want to leave. But he didn't want her to get into trouble with her mother. He took a bowl of ice cream from the fridge and sat in front of the television.

He wondered if there would be any interesting soaps on at this hour. He didn't have to look long before an advert caught his attention. He stared at the screen and blinked in disbelief. This was his dream come true. If only he could convince his parents.

Brian started rehearsing how he would phrase the question, then decided against it. He would just have to play it by ear when the time came.

The time came the following evening at dinner. His mother had outdone herself with the steak, and Brian could see that his father was in a good mood.

"You won't believe what happened to me today," Kevin said, a glint in his eye as he looked at his wife, amused.

"What?" Donna asked as she put a forkful of steak in her mouth. Kevin only got this excited when one of his investments paid a huge return.

"I saw an old high school friend, Josh. He came to my office to invite me to my class's thirtieth reunion. He wants me to go down to San Francisco next weekend," Kevin snorted, slicing his steak into pieces. "As if I have time for high school reunions."

"Your class's thirtieth reunion? That sounds exciting, hon. You should totally go. I would have loved to go with you, but I have a charity event that weekend," Donna said, smiling. The truth was she had a feeling that some of Kevin's high school friends might not be so accepting of their relationship. The opposite was true of the friends they both made at Yale. Those they kept in touch with fully supported them and embraced their relationship.

"Yeah, Dad. You should go. It'll be a blast. Besides, weren't you the star of the basketball team? They'll be bummed if you don't go..." Brian chimed in.

Kevin chuckled. "Well, since you two have already decided for me, I guess I have no choice."

"You'll thank us later," Donna beamed.

Brian waited for a few moments before he said, "Dad, I saw something really interesting on TV yesterday."

"Is that so?" Kevin replied, not looking up from his food.

"You know, I've been thinking of what to do with the remaining weeks before I go to college..."

"Hmm," Kevin muttered, not paying much attention. Donna stared at her son suspiciously.

"And I was thinking of the best way to perfect my flying and enjoy myself at the same time. You know, one last fling before I go to college..."

This time, Kevin looked up. "What are you driving at, son?"

Brian took a deep breath. *Here goes nothing.* "Well, I saw an advertisement yesterday about vacationing in Brazil, and it just blew my mind. I think I could easily fly there and stay on one of the beaches for a couple of weeks, with my friends. It would be the best vacation ever!"

"Brazil?!" Donna shrieked. "How can you think of flying so far away on your own? How would we keep an eye on you? Who knows what trouble you'll get into there?"

Kevin was thoughtful. "That's a very difficult request to make, son. Your mom's right. How do we know you won't get yourself into any trouble?"

Brian smiled. At least his father had not rejected his request outright. "Dad, I can't assure you that I won't get into any scrapes, and you know I'll do my best to stay out of trouble. I think you can trust my judgment."

"It's not been that bad so far," Kevin agreed. "But what makes you think you can fly to Brazil on your own?"

All this time, Donna was looking from one to the other, feeling like she was going to explode. "Don't tell me you're even considering this," she warned Kevin, whose facial expression was non-committal. She would not stand for it!

Brian tried to keep from grinning. It was almost too easy. "I guess the best way to convince you is for me to show you." A brief pause. "You're going to San Francisco next week, right? Why don't you let me fly you there, and then you can judge for yourself if I can fly to Brazil or not?"

Kevin pursed his lips. "Fair enough."

Donna couldn't hold it any longer. "Do you mean to tell me that you're actually taking his request seriously?" She was incredulous.

"Mom don't worry. I'm not going to do anything stupid."

"I'll be the judge of that," Kevin said curtly. Turning to his wife, "Honey, I haven't said yes yet. Besides, he has to convince me, right?"

Brian nodded, his eyes bright with hope.

Donna gave her husband a look that showed how upset she was but said nothing.

Kevin got the message. "I mean, he must convince *us*. Let's just give him a chance..."

Donna nodded, but there was no way she could feel comfortable with the idea. Her only son flying off to Brazil on his own? It was preposterous.

If it was up to her alone, she would throw his request into the wastebasket, right where it belonged. But they had agreed to put up a united front in their parenting. At least, Kevin had insisted on a trial run.

Brian looked from his mom to his dad and gave a silent cheer. He knew he had won round one.

3

Chapter 3

Rachel heard her mother's voice before she saw her. The older woman was humming an old Spanish tune that she claimed her own mother had taught her. The key turned in the latch, and the door swung open. Her mother entered the kitchen and came toward her as she made dinner.

"Something smells good in here," Sierra said, observing her daughter's movements around the kitchen.

"I'm just trying out a recipe a friend gave me. How was your day?"

"Great," Sierra replied, chewing on a biscuit from the fridge. "Actually, it was horrible. I was on my feet all day attending to customers. And then I had to go back to the office to do some typing."

Rachel clucked her tongue sympathetically. To give them the type of lifestyle she thought they deserved, her mother worked two jobs. Her father...well, he had disappeared before she could even realize she was supposed to have one.

"Mom, I told you if only you would let me work during the summer, you wouldn't have to work so hard."

Sierra shook her head emphatically. "We've been over this a thousand times, Rachel. I don't want you to work. I just want you to concentrate on your studies. I'm the mom, so I'll pay the bills."

"But mother, I can do both; read my books *and* have a job. Besides, it's not like I have anything to do all day..."

"Okay, have you found a babysitting job yet?" Sierra had told her daughter that the only job she would allow her to take would be babysitting. For some reason, she felt it was safer than the other jobs available for someone of Rachel's age, even though she was almost seventeen.

"No, but-"

"Can we have this discussion later? I'm starving," Sierra announced, effectively putting an end to the conversation.

Rachel bristled but said nothing. Though she loved her mother, she hated the fact that her mom refused to listen to her many times, especially when she had something important to say.

"Rache, I know you just want to be like the other girls," her mother said softly when they were eating. "But you're not just any girl. You're my girl, and believe me when I say I know what's best for you."

Rachel wanted to scream. This was the same thing her mother had told her when she had tried to tell her about Brian. Her mother didn't want her to have boyfriends either now or in the future, and that was the end of it. Her mother wanted her to be a lawyer, and that was it. Period. No excuses allowed.

Rachel knew her mother loved her but doubted that she always knew what was best for her. There was no point arguing with her, though, so she settled for a sigh. "Yes, mother," she muttered with resignation.

*****

Donna watched them, arms akimbo, as her husband packed his suitcase and Brian stood beside him with a self-satisfied grin on his face.

"I don't suppose I need to tell you what a bad idea this is..." she said, a resigned note in her tone.

Kevin walked up to her and kissed her on the cheek. "No, you don't."

Donna leaned over and knotted his tie. "Just be careful."

Brian grinned at her worried face. "Don't worry, Mom. I promise to bring him back to you in one piece. Alive."

She reached over and pinched his cheek, a habit Brian detested but had grown to expect. "You do that."

"Don't miss me too much," Kevin teased as he walked towards the door, glancing backwards.

"You know I will. Every second you're gone," Donna flirted, pouting her lips. She wiggled her fingers in a farewell greeting and sighed.

Brian smiled, gave his mother a wave, and followed his father out the door.

*****

Kevin was glad to see the old faces again. The whole team was there. Some of them came with their wives.

At the bar, he saw Josh, Kyle, Sean, and Adam. Josh waved him over, a big grin on his face, and the others welcomed him fondly.

"My, you're still in shape, Kevin, even after thirty years. How in the world did you do it?" Kyle asked, envious, as he sometimes struggled with his weight.

Kevin chuckled. "It's the wife. She keeps me on a healthy

regimen.”

"Cool,” Kyle mused.

"So, it's not from shooting baskets then?” Adam asked, tongue in cheek.

"I wish... Don't really get the time.”

"Maybe we should have a game this weekend,” Sean suggested.

They all nodded as they considered the idea. Josh raised a hand, assuming leadership of the group. "That's a good idea, Sean. But first, let's get reacquainted. It's been thirty years since we saw each other, and a lot of water has passed under the bridge...”

"True, true...” Sean muttered.

"I'm sure we all want to know how well we've been faring over the years,” Josh continued. The bartender dropped a cocktail in front of Kevin, and he gave an appreciative nod before lifting it to his lips. "Let's start with you, Kevin. How has life treated you so far?”

Kevin quickly gulped his drink, leaving just a remnant at the base of his glass. He beamed at his friends. "Not too badly,” he said, surveying the room. "I was accepted into Yale to study Computer Engineering. I actually met my wife there.”

"Nice!” Kyle said, sipping his drink.

Kevin chuckled, happy to have the floor. "I tried my hands on a few things for a while, until in 2002, I launched my business, and I have to say, life has been pretty good. We've paid off our mortgage, which is a huge relief.” He gulped the rest of his drink, then continued. "Donna wanted to come but could not due to prior engagements. We have a teenage son, who is my pride and joy. He's just like his old man,” he said, smiling as he looked around the group.

"Does that mean he's good at basketball too?" Kyle asked.

"Not just basketball," Kevin said. "He's good at football too. Captain of the team. But, he wants to be a pilot."

"You don't say," Josh remarked, a tinge of envy in his voice. "Well, from all indications, you appear to be living the dream, Kevin."

"Thank you," Kevin said, humbly.

The rest of the men began to talk about their lives; their wives and their children, and they made good-natured jokes about each other. However, Kevin found it hard to stay focused. He knew he was a bit conceited, but none of them were as successful as he. It seemed only Adam had the entrepreneurial spirit. He had been running his business for about five years now.

They ended the meeting with plans for a reunion basketball game the following day. Kevin strode back to his hotel, exultant. Brian was waiting for him, watching television.

"How did it go, Dad?" Brian asked.

"Son, I couldn't have imagined a better time," Kevin said, sighing contentedly. "We're having a ball game tomorrow."

"Really?" Brian asked, his eyes wide. "But you haven't played in years, Dad. Aren't you worried?"

"Maybe I should be. But then I remember that the other players haven't played in years also. It'll be fine." Kevin rested on the bed and said, "By the way, your flying was great today, son. Do the same when we're going back home, and I'll see if we can do something about your request."

"Thanks, Dad," Brian said, beaming but trying to keep the excitement from his tone. Getting his father's approval was easier than he had imagined.

*****

There were two teams on the court. Josh, Kyle, and Kevin made up one team, and Adam, Tony and Sean made up another. Their families were cheering both teams from the court side. Brian shouted as loud as the rest.

They had fun throwing the ball around, but it was even more fun when they occasionally made a basket. Brian noticed that a few of Kevin's classmates looked at him strangely, but he ignored them. He was used to it. It was one of the 'perks' of having a father who was white.

Though Kevin was a lot older, he still had some of his dribbling skills, and he put them to good use on the court. He was not named most valuable player of his basketball team for nothing, as he scored 18 out of the 22 points his team made to wind up as the winner of the game.

"You looked good out there, Dad," Brian said at the end of the game.

Kevin gave Brian a playful punch. "That's how it's played, son. That's how it's played," he said, out of breath. "The guys want to go out for a couple of drinks. You know, to celebrate our victory. Want to come?"

"Nah, Dad. It's your reunion." It would be more opportunity for the strange glances and possibly uncomfortable conversation. He didn't want his dad troubled by that. Brian had only one mission on this trip: to get his father on board with his plan to fly to Brazil.

"Nonsense, son. Let's go," Kevin insisted.

"No, really, Dad. You guys would spend most of the time making jokes I wouldn't understand anyway."

Kevin nodded slowly. "You're probably right. I'll meet you back at the hotel." And then his father did a little jog back to meet his teammates, feeling like he was young again. Brian shook his head and got out his mobile phone to call Rachel.

*****

Two days later, they were on their way home, and Kevin felt like he was invincible. It had been a great trip, not lessened by the fact that he had managed the winning basket. As he looked at Brian, he felt a sense of pride. His son's flying skills were top-notch. He took off and touched down confidently. The idea of him spending a week or two in Brazil didn't sound so preposterous after all.

"Was everything to your satisfaction, Sir?"

"Aye, Captain," Kevin said with a wink.

Brian grinned. "Glad to be of service, Sir," he said with a mock salute. He knew he had won round two. But round three was coming, and it promised to be harder than the first two.

4

Chapter 4

"What?" Craig shouted excitedly into the phone. "What did you do; promise him the whole of Wall Street or something?"

"I did no such thing. All I had to do was pass a test, which I did with flying colors," Brian replied, trying but failing to keep the self-satisfaction out of his voice.

"Way to go, man! I can't believe we're going to Brazil. Wait till I tell Tess!" Craig put his phone on speaker and scrolled through his phone, trying to see if he could send her a quick message.

Brian rolled his eyes. "Hey, I didn't say you could bring anyone along."

"I'm not bringing *anyone* along. I'm bringing Tess," Craig said decisively. He twirled his fingers. This trip was the best opportunity to get to know her better.

"Who the hell is she?"

"She's the kind of girl any red-blooded male would die for."

"Sure. Just like Trish and Lolita were. When are you going to grow up?" Brian said in mock remonstration.

"Hey, man, I'm not like you. I've got a lot of love to give, and I'm generous with it," Craig joked.

"Yeah, and a lot of heartaches to spread around too."

"Aw, shut up. The girls do that to themselves." Deciding to change the topic, Craig asked, "What did Rachel say about this? I bet she's thrilled."

"That's just the point. I don't know how I'm going to bust her out. You know, rescue her from the dragon." Brian cradled his head in his hands. He felt really helpless.

"Yeah, man. That's something. It's going to be difficult."

"Got any bright ideas?"

"Sorry, kid. This one's on you. You'll figure out something. You always do. I mean, the way you guys have been managing to smuggle dates under the dragon's ever-watchful eye is beyond me."

"You know, you are no help at all, man. I get us a plane, figure out how we can fly off in it, and you can't even come up with a simple plan to help me spring my girl..." Brian sighed in frustration.

"Loosen up, kid. You got this far. Just remember all the tricks I taught you."

"Taught me?" Brian shrieked in disbelief.

"Yeah... And now, it's time for me to sit on my butt and enjoy the fruits of my labor. Oh, and before I forget... I talked with the rest of the guys, and party is tomorrow." Craig scrolled through his phone to confirm the venue.

"What party?"

"Are you kidding? We've been talking about this for weeks. It's very important! After all, it's only our last summer party before we go to college. Anyway, it'll be at the beach. 6 pm. Don't be late."

Brian hissed in disgust and slammed down the phone. He would have to go for the stupid party as his teammates would expect him to be there. Craig was right about one thing, though; he was going to find a way to take Rachel along with him if it was the last thing he did.

*****

The party was in the typical Craig style; loud, wild, and swinging. The music was deafening, and scantily clad bodies gyrated to it. Brian gulped as he watched a group of boys passing a white substance among themselves. He had promised his dad he would never touch that stuff.

"Don't you think they could keep it down a little?" Rachel said, holding on to Brian's hand and wrinkling her nose in disgust.

"If they did, then it wouldn't be Craig's party," Brian replied pragmatically.

As if on cue, Craig started heading towards them with a redhead in tow. She looked like she was angry about something.

"Hi, guys. You're late," he said, slapping Brian on the back. "Party's already started."

"Yeah, I can see that," Brian piped.

Craig pretended not to take notice of the sarcastic remark and said, "You guys, meet Tess, the girl I was telling you about."

"Nice to meet you," Brian greeted with a small smile.

Rachel nodded at the pretty redhead, but Tess just stared at them and smacked on a wad of chewing gum rather loudly. She was wearing a skin-tight, leather skirt with a crop top and dark lipstick. Brian had no idea what Craig saw in the girl.

Craig, a bit embarrassed, grabbed Tess's hand and said, "Well, we'll be seeing you two. You guys enjoy the party."

"That girl's rather rude, don't you think?" Rachel asked Brian as they tried to find a spot on the dance floor.

"Yeah, she's a real piece of work. How are we going to cope with that kind of girl for two weeks?"

Rachel gave him a suspicious look. "What are you talking about?"

"Well, who would have thought it? My dad has finally given me the go-ahead to fly to Brazil, and you, Craig, and his new girlfriend are coming with me."

"Really?" Rachel's expression brightened. Then, just as quickly, her face fell. "I'm happy for you, Brian, but you know that's not possible. I had to tell my mother that I was going to Lizzie's to study tonight, just to be able to come to the party. She'd never let me out of her sight for two weeks. You'd just have to go without me."

"Don't even think about it, Rach," he protested, putting a finger to her lips. "You're going with me; we'll figure out a way." He held her close to him as the music slowed.

When the music changed again, Rachel excused herself to go to the bathroom.Brian scanned the crowd aimlessly until his eyes spotted a young man standing about two meters away from him. He recognized him.

The guy worked in the school office and happened to owe him five hundred dollars. From the looks of it, this guy would not be able to pay him till they finished high school. On impulse, he began moving towards him. Maybe, somehow, he could work this to his advantage.

*****

"Need I ask where you've been?" Mary Tolbert asked as her daughter staggered into the living room at 1 am. She was obviously soused.

"Out," Tess said curtly.

"You've been drinking again, Tess. Haven't you?"

Tess gave a sigh of infinite patience. "Mom, we've been over this. I'm not a kid anymore. I'm not one of your second graders." Why wouldn't her mom understand that she was an adult? She was nearly eighteen.

"Well, you certainly are acting like one," Mary retorted, her voice shrill.

Tess gave another drawn-out sigh. "Where's Francis?"

"Asleep, just as you should be," Mary answered.

"I'm going to bed, Mom. You should too."

Without waiting for a response, Tess left the living room and went to her room. Mary's mouth hung open, like she wanted to say something, but she clamped it shut. Fighting back tears, she put off the TV and went to bed.

*****

"Craig!" his mother called out good-naturedly when he sauntered in at half-past one. Patricia was watching a late-night action movie. She loved how the hero never died even if everyone else did and the death defying stunts. Irrespective of how tired she felt, she made sure to watch an action movie almost every night.

"A little late tonight aren't we, Craig?" she asked, smiling indulgently at him.

"I'm sorry about that, Mom," he said while bending to kiss her on the cheek. He settled into a seat next to her favorite armchair and turned to her. "Mom, I want to tell you something... But first, promise you'll be cool..."

"Tell me first..." Patricia replied hesitantly.

"I was invited to go to Brazil on vacation for two weeks," he announced with glee.

"Craig, going on vacation may be all well and good, but you know things have been rather tight, what with the restaurant and the bills-"

"Mom, you don't need to worry about money. Brian's taking me. It's an all-expense-paid trip!"

"Well, then, good for you."

"The neatest part about it is that Brian will be flying us to Brazil."

"You don't say... Is he so good at flying?"

"Very," Craig asserted.

"Well, I won't stop you from going and having fun. Just make sure to call me every day," Patricia said.

"You got it!"

Craig climbed up the stairs to his bedroom with an extra bounce in his step and a wide, lip-splitting grin.

*****

Rachel sighed sadly when Brian came to see her two days later. "It's great that you've finally figured out a way to fly into the sunset. I just wish you could figure out a way for us to go together..."

"And what if I told you I have? We'll just ask your mom."

"That's your *great* idea?" Rachel was incredulous. "There's no way my mom's ever going to let me go."

"Don't be too sure of that. What if the school asks her to let you take this trip?" Brian grinned.

"What are you talking about?" she demanded.

Brian fished around in his pocket and produced an official-looking envelope, then gingerly opened it and produced an official-looking letter. Rachel grabbed it from his hands and eagerly scanned it. Then she let out a whoop.

"I can't believe this!" she cried. "Brian Anderson, what on Earth did you do?"

He touched her cheek. "Darling, you know I've always been a genius..."

She punched him on the elbow. "Brian, cut the crap, and tell me exactly what you did."

"Aw, that hurts," he said, wincing in mock pain. "You're going to have to kiss that to make it better."

"Brian..." Rachel threatened.

"Alright, alright. I had a guy, who owed me a favor. It turned out the school secretary owed him one too. So, to even out favors, I came up with this brilliant plan. And tada!" he said, spreading his arms dramatically.

"I can't believe you did all that just to get me to go," Rachel mused in disbelief.

"I had to, babe. But all in all, it was just a case of, you know, one good turn deserving another," Brian said sheepishly.

Impulsively, Rachel threw her arms around him and hugged him. "Brian, you really are a genius."

"That I am. So, how soon can you pack?"

"That depends on how soon I can finish shopping," Rachel said, winking.

Brian gave a mock groan, but Rachel ignored him.

"You know, Brian," she said huskily, moving closer to him.

"What?"

"I think I owe you a favor," she muttered, straightening his shirt. "You know, one good turn..."

Brian swallowed, his heart thumping in anticipation. "And what would that be?"

"This..." she said, cupping his face with her lips puckered.

29

As he leaned down for the kiss, Brian realized he had won round three. He imagined a drum roll in his head.

Let the party begin; or in this case, the journey...

5

Chapter 5

I f there was one thing the Andersons knew about traveling, it was how to do so in style. They had a family vacation each year, and they always shopped vigorously for it. If it was summer, they had their entire summer gear: bikinis, shorts, tank tops, lots of towels, and sunscreen. If it was winter, they were like the Boy Scouts; always prepared with gloves, mittens, scarves, hats, coats, mufflers – the works.

This tradition of getting properly geared for a trip had become a part of Brian. Even though the trip would last barely two weeks, he knew he needed a whole new summer wardrobe. So, he called Craig, picked up Rachel, and they all decided to go to the mall. Shopping online was all well and good, but they didn't have that much time left, and Rachel always liked trying out her outfits in the stores before she bought them.

"Rache, please, we're not going to spend all day here," Brian pleaded when they got to the clothing section.

"What do you mean?" Rachel asked, sounding indignant, her hands on her hips.

"Look, I'm sorry. What I mean is, let's try not to spend more than an hour here, okay?" Brian said, running his hand through his hair.

"You're acting as if I'm the only one going shopping. Aren't you guys going to get some things too?"

"Sure, we will..." Craig said. "But, since we're not too particular, we're likely to finish shopping before you do."

"Really? We'll see about that," Rachel replied, a determined look on her face.

"Let's meet back here in an hour then."

Craig's jaw dropped, before he picked it up and chuckled. "Look, he's kidding. Take all the time you need."

"I need just one hour," Rachel said sweetly, then she walked away from them towards the mannequins. Brian shook his head in exasperation as he watched her.

Craig gave his friend a playful shove. "Not cool, dude. You shouldn't have said anything."

"I know Rachel. If I didn't say anything, we'll spend at least five hours in here."

"Well, what I know is that you're gonna regret this. She won't forgive you easily."

Brian just shook his head as they headed towards their section of the mall. Thirty minutes later, the boys had finished shopping. Their bags were bulging with shorts and trunks, water skis, sunglasses; everything they thought they would need for a summer trip.

"Think she's nearly finished?" Craig asked after they made their last purchases.

"Not a chance."

"Then, there's nothing to stop us from playing a video game before she's through..."

"Are you sure you really want to play a game with me?"

"What do you mean?"

"Cause you're only gonna lose!" Brian taunted.

Craig made a mock expression of sadness and said, "Man, I really feel sorry for you. You're gonna take it so hard when you lose."

*****

Forty-five minutes later, when they had each won a round, Craig peeked at the clock. "Oops. I think we might have kept somebody waiting," he said.

"I doubt it. But let's go and find her anyway."

They ambled towards the ladies' section, and sure enough, Rachel was standing by the info desk, waiting for them and tapping her foot impatiently.

"Where were you guys?" she asked when she saw them. "I've been waiting for you for over fifteen minutes."

"Sorry," Brian said.

"We were sort of held up," Craig tried to explain.

"Why didn't you call us though?" Brian asked. "We would have come immediately."

"I wanted to give you a little more time to finish your shopping," she said, smiling at them. But it did not reach her eyes.

Brian and Craig exchanged a look but said nothing. Then Craig noticed something.

"Rachel, where are your bags?" he asked.

"Oh, that. I didn't find anything I liked, so I didn't buy anything," Rachel said, turning her face away.

"What?" Brian was incredulous. "In this huge mall? How can you not find anything you like?"

"You see, that's the problem," Rachel said, facing him. "You said it yourself: the mall is huge. How do you expect me to find what I like in one hour?"

Brian glanced at Craig, who mouthed, "Uh-oh."

Brian took a deep breath and said, "Okay, Rache. You know what, forget what I said earlier. Take your time and find exactly what you want. We won't rush you."

Rachel squealed and gave him a hug. "Thanks, Brian. You're the best."

She ran back to the mannequins.

"Well, there goes our football game," Brian muttered, defeated.

"*Our?* What do you mean by 'our'? Do I have to stay too?" Craig objected in a high-pitched voice.

"Oh, come on, buddy. You can't leave me alone here. Besides, it will be no fun if you watch the game alone. We'll watch the reruns together."

Just then, Rachel came running towards them. "Hey, guys. I think I need your help. I'm going to try some dresses on, and you're going to tell me if they look great or not so that I can make up my mind faster on what to choose."

Brian and Craig shrugged then followed her. Three and a half hours later, they all left the mall.

As Brian dropped Rachel and Craig off, he told them, "Remember, we meet at my house tomorrow. 8 am. Don't be late. Tell your girl, Craig."

"Don't worry, Brian. She'll be ready."

*****

The next day, after a long time in weeks, Brian woke up before the sun. He still had some last-minute packing to do. Before he finished packing his second suitcase, his father called him and pressed something into his hand. It was a pack of condoms.

"Now, son, I don't want you doing anything stupid out there. But if you do, protect yourself," his father said sternly.

Brian took one look at it and gulped. Then he glanced at his father and nodded weakly.

Donna crushed Brian to her bosom that morning when she saw him. The trip to San Francisco had gone smoothly, and she had been won over to the idea of him going on holiday and flying on his own. He certainly deserved it.

"Stay out of trouble, honey," she told him. "And make sure you call the minute you're there. Okay?"

Brian nodded obediently, even though he just wanted to tell her to stop fretting. "You know I will, Mom," he said, giving her a peck on the cheek. He would miss his parents.

The rest of the group got to his house early. Well, except for Tess, who was ten minutes late.

"Okay, since we're all here, I think we should take off. Our ride's waiting." Brian had taken the liberty of hiring a limo to take them and their luggage to the airport.

"Man, this is so cool..." Craig said when they saw the limo.

"You never cease to surprise me, Brian Anderson," Rachel quipped, giving him a kiss. Only Tess appeared unaffected by Brian's gesture and looked around them as if she was used to riding in limos every day.

Without much fuss, they piled themselves and their luggage into the limo to start their journey. Once they were in the car, Brian connected his phone to the car's dashboard and played 'Ridin' by Chamillionaire all the way to the airport.

*****

Rachel glanced at Tess, who sat beside her as they drove to the airport, and she didn't like what she saw. Tess wore another too short, too tight skirt, with loud make-up. And although she had not spoken to them at the party, it appeared now that she had a sharp tongue too. Rachel wondered what on Earth Craig saw in her.

Tess, also, was coolly appraising Rachel, who sat demurely, her hands tucked in her lap and her lips twisted in a sneer. This Rachel might think she was too good for the rest of them, but Tess was determined to show her who was boss.

Out of the corner of his eye, Brian warily observed them watching each other and smiled. There were few things he liked more than a good catfight. Tess looked tough and like she might explode any minute, but Rachel had a will of steel. He was putting his money on Rachel, of course.

When they got inside the plane, Rachel watched as Tess chatted about how she was going to buy such a plane for herself someday. *In your dreams*, Rachel thought.

The guys quickly went inside and headed straight for the bar. Rachel followed them.

"No drinking while flying, guys," she said, shaking her head.

"Aw, come on, Rache. It's only a couple of beers," Brian said, looking sheepish.

"We promise we'll be on our best behavior," Craig added.

"No!" Rachel insisted. They weren't even legally old enough to drink yet but Craig always found a way to get them alcohol.

Tess came up behind them and supported the guys. "Yeah, give it a rest. Or are you afraid of just a few drinks?" she sneered at Rachel.

Rachel felt her face reddening; she hated being made to feel like a wimp. Ignoring Tess, she turned to Brian and said, "Brian, you're in charge of this plane. I trust you to do the right thing. There'll be plenty of time for drinks when we land."

Brian sighed. "You're right," he said in defeat.

"I'm not flying the plane," Craig said. "So, I can have one beer."

He was about to pick one of the beer cans, but Brian stopped him. "You're my co-pilot."

Craig grimaced and sighed before following Brian to the cockpit to take his place beside him. Tess glanced over in Rachel's direction and mockingly muttered, "Yes, ma'am."

Rachel could feel the heat in her face. "One of us has to be cautious, you know?" she retorted.

"Of course, ma'am. Whatever you say, ma'am," Tess continued to mock.

Rachel sighed, walked down the aisle to find a comfortable seat, and tried her best to ignore Tess' attempts to get under her skin. Tess wasn't worth getting angry over. Instead, she listened as Brian gave them instructions on how to strap themselves in their seats.

"Alright, guys. Are we ready to go?" Brian called out about ten minutes later.

"Let's get going," Tess responded.

"Go, go!" Rachel piped.

"Aye, aye, Captain," Craig grinned at his friend.

"Then, get ready for the ride of your life," Brian said as he began take-off.

6

Chapter 6

Rachel peered out of her window, exhilarated by the scenery around her. She could see that they were leaving the city, and it had never looked more beautiful to her. Tiny houses were arranged neatly along winding roads, and neighborhoods were separated by large patches of green. She was in awe of the cloud formations they passed through.

For a fleeting moment, she felt guilty about lying to her mother about the trip. Her mom deserved a vacation, as she was always working. She sank in her seat and rummaged in her bag for some nuts. The cabin felt cool and was quiet, soothing her to sleep. She closed her eyes, hoping to doze off, then she heard a stomping noise behind her.

Rachel turned to look at Tess, who had her headphones on and was wildly shaking her head and stamping her feet, no doubt to the music she was listening to. She grimaced in annoyance. Tess felt Rachel's eyes on her and turned to face her.

"What are you looking at?" she asked with venom, removing her headphones.

Rachel smiled. "Oh, nothing. I was just wondering..." she

shrugged.

"Wondering what?" Tess asked, her eyes narrowing.

"Well, it's actually none of my business," Rachel replied sweetly, "but it's just that...you know, Craig and Brian have been friends a long time, and Craig has always had a profusion of girlfriends..."

"So?" Tess raised a quizzical brow.

"Well, after seeing Craig with his many girlfriends, I began to notice something, a sort of trend..." Rachel paused and glanced at Tess' face. "I don't think you're ready to hear it."

"Out with it," Tess snapped, clenching her teeth.

"Okay, you asked for it. Well, Craig always seems to prefer girls who have a little class or, you know, are a little bit sophisticated. Such girls have more of a chance with Craig. But the brassy, sassy ones just tickle his fancy for a while, and then he gets rid of them. He just *loved* having them around, I guess for his ego... But after a while, they bore him."

Tess bristled with anger. "You're right. It's none of your business!"

"Just trying to give you a little tip; if you want to last long with Craig, learn to act like a lady." Rachel said, smiling sweetly all the while.

Tess saw red. She looked like she was about to burst a vessel. "Oh, you think you know everything, don't you? You don't know a thing about Craig. You might think you're better than the rest of us, but you're nothing but a stuck-up, sneaky b—"

"Is everything all right in there?" Craig called out from the cockpit. "Are you two bonding or something?"

"It couldn't be better," Rachel responded, folding her arms. "Tess and I are discovering we have a lot of things in common."

Tess' face hardened as she sat back. Her right temple throbbed as she burned with rage, but she thought better of acting on it. At least not now...on this plane. Wait till they get to land; Rachel would regret that she made an enemy out of her. She clamped her mouth shut and stared out of the window instead.

Rachel settled down in her seat and looked out of the window on the opposite side, determined to enjoy the flight and the scenery.

*****

"What do you suppose they're doing in there?" Brian asked his friend without taking his eyes off the controls that displayed the aircraft's position.

"I don't know. Rachel said they're discovering they have some things in common," Craig replied, running his hands over the controls, thrilled to be flying autopilot with his friend.

"I doubt it," Brian said. "They're as different as night and day." He glanced at his friend, who was munching on some Cheerios. "Are you serious about her, Craig?"

"What?" Craig muttered, preoccupied. "Oh, Tess... Sure."

"Really? Do you think you could go out with her for a year?"

"A year? That's an awfully long time, man."

"Not long enough if you're serious about someone," Brian said sternly.

"Quit the lecture, man. You'll develop premature gray in your hair." Suddenly, he tipped his head to the side. "Hey, what's this?" he asked, running his hands over a strange-looking contraption.

"That's the radio. We can use it to call the nearest control tower if we get into trouble."

"Wow, that's cool." He put it on and began to scream. "Mayday, mayday-"

"Give me that!" Brian snapped, grabbing it from him and turning it off. "It's meant for distress signals, not something you can goof around with."

Craig was taken aback by his friend's anger. "Take it easy, man. I was just trying to test it."

"Just like you tend to try out everything about your life instead of taking it seriously," Brian retorted.

Craig started to say something in response then thought better of it. He wondered if Brian had a point. It was true that he didn't take life too seriously, but was that affecting the important things in his life? Perhaps he could do with goofing around less, he thought.

Brian felt uncomfortable after snapping at Craig, but he was tired of his friend's nonchalance, and he wouldn't be a good friend if he didn't tell him what needed changing in his life.

They continued the trip in silence, each pretending to admire the view outside.

*****

Brian felt pretty good as he handled the controls. He had never felt more proud than he did in this moment, flying his friends to another country. He glanced at Craig, whose eyelids were beginning to flutter. He looked very sleepy. Brian shook his head. Some first pilot he was turning out to be. Brian checked the dashboard again and realized he needed to increase his altitude and speed to avoid the clouds looming in front of him.

As Brian slowly increased the plane's altitude, he heard a loud thud, like the plane had struck something hard. Had he come in contact with something? He tried the controls. He needed to escape but could not increase the plane's altitude further no matter what he did. From the sound of things, it seemed

41

like there was something inside the engine. His instructors had warned him about bird strikes, which were a nightmare for any pilot. They were losing engine power fast.

He frantically pressed the controls before grabbing the radio and turning it on. "Mayday, mayday..."

Craig was startled awake. He had dozed off for a little while. "What's going on?" he asked anxiously, blinking to drive sleep away.

Brian ignored him. "Mayday, mayday..." he continued to shout. He was getting a faint, distorted signal and could not make out what they said.

Just then, the plane lurched and began to descend.

Rachel unstrapped herself and went to the cockpit. "What's going on?"

"It looks like we're going down!" Tess shouted, sounding scared and worried.

As if in response, the plane lurched again.

Rachel tried to get a hold of Brian, even as she was tossed about by the unstable plane. "What are we going to do?" she cried.

Brian didn't know. It seemed that birds had also damaged the fuel tank as he could see that the fuel level was dropping. He knew he had filled the tank before they left. The plane lurched again, and he used all his maneuvering skills to get it away from the mountains they would certainly have crashed into.

He took a deep breath and tried to think. *Focus*, he told himself. He had to regain control of the plane. He knew what he had to do.

"Alright, everybody, back in your seats. I'm going to find someplace safe to land."

Rachel and Tess hurried away like scared rabbits. Brian tried once again to speak to the control tower. He could only hear a crackling noise.

"Mayday, I have had a bird strike, and I am experiencing engine failure. I'm going to make an attempt to land." Through the radio, he sent his coordinates. He hoped his message would get through to them and make it easier for them to be found once they landed.

Craig watched the figures and cried out in a panicked voice, "We're falling! A thousand feet above sea level!"

Brian ignored him and tried to remember everything he had learned about emergency landing. The plane lurched again and bumped him against the control panel.

"Nine hundred feet..." Craig read out in horror. This was no joke! Brian was trying to maneuver the plane, and it looked like they were going to land in a forest of some kind. It wouldn't do to land among the trees, Craig thought to himself. "Six hundred feet..."

He would have to find a clearing, Brian thought frantically. Even above the roar of the engine, he could hear Rachel's sobbing and Tess' shouts.

"Four hundred feet..." Craig whined.

Brian thought he could see something, a small clearing. But could they get there in time?

"Three hundred feet..."

No time now. They would have to wing it, he decided and threw the plane into full throttle. He joined the other three in screaming as the plane headed for the area of green. Brian saw a myriad of colors: green, red, and blue. Then all was black.

7

Chapter 7

Brian could hear someone calling him from what seemed like miles away. Opening his eyes, he could hardly see a thing. Then he could make out Craig's silhouette standing over him. He realized he was bathed in a cloud of dust, and he was awkwardly strapped in his seat. He released the strap and fell to the ground, wincing as a headache took hold. There was a stinging sensation on the side of his head. When he touched it, he felt something wet and sticky. Blood.

"That looks nasty," Craig said as he inspected the wound. Craig could see that blood was oozing from it. "It doesn't look too deep though. We will just need something to stop the blood."

Brian tried to stand up and noticed that Craig was holding his arm gingerly. "Looks like you were banged up as well." He said, his voice sounding like a croak.

Craig shrugged. "It looks worse than it is."

"What about the girls?" Brian asked, worried. He had to find Rachel.

"Let's check the cabin," Craig suggested.

As they began to walk through the cabin, Brian felt sort of

light-headed, and he held on to the side of the plane that hadn't fallen in. After a while, the feeling subsided, and he felt steady on his feet. His injury stung, but his headache had dulled a little.

They both moved gingerly, using Brian's flashlight, which had been in his pocket, thankfully. Suddenly, Brian stumbled on something on the ground. He bent down to check what it was and discovered a body lying face down, with another a few feet away. Flashlight in hand, he turned the person over. Relief flooded him at the sight. Rachel...

He shook her. "Rachel," he called. She groaned and opened her eyes.

"Where am I?" she asked, disoriented. She tried to get up.

Brian supported her. "Take it easy. You might be hurt. We're in a forest somewhere," he told her as she sat up. He gave her a quick appraisal. "How do you feel?"

"My ankle... I think I might have fallen on it," Rachel replied. "But otherwise, I'm fine."

Brian sighed in relief. "I'm glad you're okay."

Craig went over to the other prone body, who was beginning to groan softly. Turning the flashlight on her, he saw that Tess also had a cut on her arm. It didn't look too bad, though. "Tess," he called to her as he shook her.

"Brian, you're hurt," Rachel murmured, finally seeing the cut on Brian's head and reaching around to see if she could find her handkerchief.

Tess sat up, wincing in pain and murmuring under her breath.

"We've gotta get out of here and get help," Rachel said, beginning to get agitated. She couldn't find her handkerchief.

Tess hugged Craig. She inspected his wound when he winced. "That doesn't look good."

Brian was glad he could use some of the first aid training he had learnt when he was a scout. He knew the first thing was to try and stop the bleeding. He tried to recall where he'd seen the first-aid kit. It would be useful to have that handy so they could prevent infection.

"There's a first-aid kit in the cockpit. I'm going to go get it," Brian said. "In the meantime, use this..." He tore part of his shirt and gave it to Tess to use as a bandage for Craig's wound. "This should stop the bleeding." He cut smaller strips for himself and Tess, to bind their own wounds.

Moments later, he returned, solemn. "I couldn't find it..." he sighed.

"It's okay, babe. It's too dark and stuffy here. We can come back later... We just need to get out of this plane."

Brian swallowed. "Okay." Perhaps they could make do with washing their wounds with clean water later.

When everyone was on their feet, they made their way out of the plane; Craig supporting Tess, and Brian supporting Rachel.

*****

It appeared to be late dusk when they went outside. They seemed to be in a forest of some kind. Brian glanced at his watch. Just after six o'clock.

"What are we going to do?" Rachel asked, in a small voice, as they all looked at the sea of green surrounding them. The foliage was thick and deep. The silence around them was eerie. She shivered.

Tess scoffed. "Well, I can tell you one thing for sure; we should be scared. We're out here in the middle of nowhere, in the jungle. There's no network, and there's no one around for miles. We're probably never going to get out of here alive!"

"Tess!" Brian and Craig cried in unison.

"We've got to face reality," Tess retorted.

"Tess, your kind of talk is the last thing we need right now," Craig replied, sounding exasperated.

"Yeah, Tess. We need to find solutions, not create more problems for ourselves," Brian added.

"You're being very unhelpful here," Rachel chastised.

Feeling insulted, Tess took menacing steps towards Rachel. "Well, look here, Miss Prim and Proper. Your boyfriend got us into this mess, and you are going to learn- Ouch!" she exclaimed as her foot struck something hard between them.

Craig walked up to her and bent down to pick it up. It was a black, leather-bound book.

"What is it?" the rest of them asked as they crowded around it.

Tess grabbed the book from Craig and opened it to the first page. It had a few sentences that seemed handwritten but were written in ancient-looking script and bold letters.

"What does it say?" Rachel asked.

Tess read aloud: "***You are about to embark on the journey of a lifetime. This journey will either destroy you or build you. Many have gone ahead of you but have failed to reach their destination. If you want to get to the end of your journey, this book must be your only compass.***"

Tess leafed through the other pages, but they were blank. "What crap!" she spat in disgust. "What sick person could have left such a weird book here?"

"Let me see," Rachel said, trying to grab it from Tess.

Craig got a hold of it first. "It sure does sound weird," he said, fingering the pages of the book with a frown. "Somebody's idea of a joke...?" he asked as he passed it on to Brian.

"I don't know. Maybe it's a guide book of some sort. Maybe a geographer left it."

Rachel grabbed it from him and examined it. She began leafing through the pages.

"Here," she said excitedly, "there's more: '**Turn east and head for the water. For in the water, you will find life.**'"

"So, what are we supposed to do with that?" Tess asked, bemused.

"I don't know. I think we should give it a try," Rachel said, turning to Brian.

"You've got to be kidding me," Tess balked.

Brian sighed. "Rachel, we don't know anything about this book. What makes you think it's going to help us or that it has anything to do with us?"

"Well, do you have anything better to suggest? What else are we going to do?" Rachel posed, holding the book close to her chest.

"It'd be a nice fairy tale if this book would help us get out of here," Craig chimed in. "You know, like Jumanji. But that's what it is, a fairy tale..."

"Tell you what we're going to do; we've got to find a way to set up a smoke signal so that any passing plane would see us and come rescue us," Brian proposed.

"How are we going to do that?" Rachel asked.

Craig smiled. "Don't worry. Brian and I know how to do these things." He turned to Brian. "It'll be just like summer camp, won't it?"

"Yeah, just that this is the real thing. Craig, we've got to go get some bamboo to build us a shelter and then make a fire."

"And what are we supposed to do while you two go get the bamboo?" Tess asked anxiously, her heart racing at the thought of being left alone in that place. It was getting darker by the minute, and insects were buzzing all about them. She feared what else might be out there. She waved her hand to swipe a mosquito from her face.

"You two will sit tight and stay put," Brian ordered.

"But, how long will you be gone?" Rachel fretted. She put the book down beside her and hastily applied her insect-repellent cream, glad she had thought to pack it.

Brian kissed her on the forehead. "Baby, we'll be right back. I promise."

Turning to Craig, he motioned for them to leave. Craig turned and waved at Tess before following beside Brian. They headed north.

Tess and Rachel sat on the grass, a few feet away from each other, not daring to think about what the next few hours would bring. Tess longed for Rachel's repellent cream but dared not ask. She looked around, instead, for something to fan herself with. Rachel drew her knees to her chest and began brooding.

*****

They walked deeper into the forest, each brandishing pocket knives, which they used to slash at the undergrowth, but it wasn't very effective. They didn't speak until Craig broke the silence after they had walked ten minutes.

"I've got a bad feeling about this," Craig said as they inched deeper still.

"What do you mean?" Brian said sharply, too sharply. The hairs on the back of his neck prickled, and he felt uneasy, but he wanted to ignore it.

Just behind them, there was the unmistakable sound of an animal's growl.

"What was that?" Craig asked.

49

"Whatever it was, you can bet it's nothing good," Brian said grimly. "Let's stand still for a few minutes. Maybe it'll go away."

"I say we make a run for it..."

"Hold your horses, Craig. If we run, we could easily become dead meat. This thing knows the jungle better than we do."

So, they hid under some bushes and waited.

*****

Half a mile away, the girls waited. With the setting of the sun came a cool wind, adding to their discomfort. The breeze also caused the leaves to rustle, increasing their anxiety. Any slight sound caused their hearts to race, and they inched ever closer together.

Rachel tried to make conversation with Tess, anything to get her mind off her fears. "Where do you think the boys might be now? Do you think they're coming back already?" she chatted nervously.

Before Tess could give her a caustic reply, a coyote howled somewhere in the distance. Rachel shuddered. Tess slapped her arm in a bid to kill a mosquito.

"Here," Rachel said, realizing her mistake. She offered Tess her small tube of insect repellent. "Rub it sparingly. We don't know how long we'll need it."

Tess looked at her, hesitated, and replied. "I'm fine, thanks."

Okay... Rachel thought. At least she tried. She wrapped her arms around her legs and rocked, frightened when she heard the howl of the coyote again. "Where in heaven's name are those boys?" she cried.

Tess shifted her weight on the small rock stool she'd found. She also was beginning to wonder where the boys were too.

What a nightmare this was turning out to be.

*****

"How long do we wait?" Craig whispered, trying to peer into the forest after they had waited about fifteen minutes. He couldn't see if the jaguar was still there or not.

"Shh. We'll double back to the girls soon," Brian said.

"How soon? They'll be worried sick by now. I say we take a chance and go now," Craig whispered fiercely.

"Okay. We'll go now. Let me check if it's still there."

Brian tip-toed forward and checked carefully. It was getting very dark, and he didn't want to use his flashlight to call attention to them. As far as he could see, the jaguar had gone.

So much for going to get bamboo. They would have to do that tomorrow. He motioned to Craig that they should get going. They crouched forward slowly, taking care not to make any sound.

Brian felt as if something was following them, stopping when they stopped and moving when they did, but he resisted the urge to look back. They were both tense, and as they got closer to the spot they had left the girls, their hearts began to beat a little faster. They moved a few more paces, and behind them came the unmistakable growl of the jaguar.

Brian and Craig stopped dead in their tracks and turned slightly to see what was behind them. The creature was stalking them! They could see it almost clearly. It was looking right at them. They could see its glowing eyes against the darkness of the early evening. Then suddenly, it turned away from them and walked slowly away.

Brian and Craig stared in disbelief after it, then they began to run.

*****

Rachel had tried so hard to be brave, but it was harder than she had bargained for. She wiped tears off her sleeve, as she thought about her mother, who would be so sad and disappointed when she found out what she had done. And Brian? What in the world could have happened to keep him so long?

Tess stared into the distance, a scowl on her face, wondering why things had to get so complicated. All they wanted to do was have fun. It was why she had agreed to go out with Craig in the first place, because he seemed like so much fun. When he had told her about the trip, she had jumped at the chance. She had wanted to get away from her overbearing mother and her *perfect* brother who could never do anything wrong.

The plane crash, and now, being lost, seemed like cruel and unusual punishment. She would never admit it openly, but despite their differences, she missed her family. She really wished she had stayed home with them, and then she could have avoided this mess. Although they weren't close, they were the only people who cared for her and would be upset if anything happened to her.

The girls heard some rustling in the bushes and, for a moment, were worried that the coyotes had cornered them. However, they were relieved when they could make out Craig's and Brian's silhouettes.

"Brian!" Rachel cried, elated. She ran to hug him. He was perspiring, and he hugged her back in relief. Tess also got up to hug Craig, glad he was still alive.

"What the hell took you guys so long?" Tess asked, a bit indignant. After all, they had come back empty-handed.

"We were so worried," Rachel added.

Brian stroked her hair. "We were almost killed by a jaguar."

"A jaguar?" Rachel gasped and shuddered. She didn't want to ask any more questions. She buried her head in Brian's shoulder.

"That must have been something. I'm glad you guys could escape," Tess said, smiling. She patted Craig's arm.

"I guess we can't light a fire tonight. We have to get some stuff from the plane and find someplace to sleep," Craig said.

"Just what I was about to suggest. Thank God we brought those sleeping bags. Rache, any food?" Brian asked.

"There are about three bags of Cheerios and peanuts, that's if they weren't ruined by the crash," she replied. "Wait, I'll come with you." She couldn't bear to be apart from him a moment longer. She could also do with a break from Tess.

Brian and Rachel went into the plane with his flashlight. The plane was on its side, so it was hard to move around it. The tail-end of the plane, where their luggage was, was the worst hit, by the looks of things, but it was still hard to tell the extent of the damage. That they were alive, and without any major injuries, was truly a miracle.

They went in search again for the first-aid-kit but had no luck. They found only two sleeping bags and a blanket. They salvaged a bag of peanuts and a couple of drinks; the rest of the food was ruined. They would have to make do.

The peanuts and the drinks did little to satisfy their hunger nor quench their thirst. In their irritation, tempers were short. The ordeal was taking its toll.

Rachel offered Brian her insect repellent, and he eagerly rubbed it all over his body.

"Hey... We have to manage that. It's all I have," she snapped.

"I'm sorry...just too many mosquitoes. I'm sure we'll be out of here tomorrow, and I'll buy you more. Don't worry!"

"Let me have that," Craig snatched the cream from Brian

before he could finish it. Rachel sighed. She watched as he squeezed the last of the tube before discarding the cream carelessly on the ground.

"You can say 'thank you,' you know..." she muttered, annoyed.

Craig raised his brow. "Seriously?!"

"What did you expect?" Tess hissed.

Noticing that Rachel wanted to retort, Brian pulled her away. "Leave it alone... Please. It's not worth it."

Craig began to clear the area where they would put the sleeping bags. Tess went over to him.

"Craig, give them to me," she said, taking the sleeping bags from his hands. "I think we should move the sleeping bags closer to this side." She pulled the sleeping bags up closer to where the plane was. She was really worried about sleeping in the open especially since the guys had said they had seen a jaguar. She wanted Craig to put the bags closer to the plane so they could have a hiding place if an animal came nearby, but she wasn't about to voice that fear.

"Why would you do that?" Craig asked. "Moving it towards the plane is stupid because we don't know how unsteady it is. It could completely combust at any moment."

Tess felt her face burn. "Don't call me stupid!" she snapped.

He wrestled the bags from her. "Then don't say stupid things."

He took the sleeping bags back to the previous spot he had wanted to place them on. Tess moved away from him, upset, but kept quiet as she watched him lay the bags out. Rachel watched her, also quiet as Brian rubbed her arm.

It was hard for them to hide their fear of the unknown. Were they going to survive this?

The sleeping bags were dusty, but they managed to crawl in; one by one, two to a bag. Rachel snuggled close to Brian, and he couldn't help thinking that under better circumstances and appropriate conditions, he would have used what his father had given him. But that would have to wait.

He thought over the events of the day. The bird strike could not have been predicted, and the damage to the plane on a cursory glance appeared extensive. He could only hope that the control tower had heard his frantic message and were busy trying to locate them.

Whatever had happened, Brian knew they had to find a way to get out of the jungle. Coyotes howled in the distance, and bodies shifted restlessly. They all found it difficult to sleep, each of them eagerly waiting for morning to come.

8

Chapter 8

Brian felt something wet on his face. He stirred in his
sleep. Could it be a dog that was licking him? He had
not had one since he was five.

He opened his eyes and realized that dew was falling, and
that was what had been softly caressing his face. He could still
feel a throbbing on the side of his head. But there was no more
bleeding. The others stirred around him. Craig stretched, then
winced at the pain in his arm. Tess wriggled out of the sleeping
bag. Rachel opened her eyes slowly and stared round in wonder.

The sun was just starting to rise, and the jungle looked so
beautiful. It certainly looked less frightening that it had the day
before. Rachel wished she had brought her camera so she could
take a picture of the sky over the jungle. There was pink, purple,
and a touch of green, which formed a masterpiece. Even Tess
couldn't hide her appreciation of the beauty surrounding them
as she gently rubbed her arm.

"Wow," she breathed. "Take a load of that."

All too soon, the sky turned blue again, and the sun came out
in all its brilliance. They sat on their sleeping bags.

"So, where do we go from here?" Rachel asked, massaging her ankle before clutching the book hopefully.

Brian sighed. He scanned the horizon. "Looks like we have to go east."

"Surely, you don't mean you want to follow that thing in Rachel's hand?" Tess posed, incredulous.

"No, it's nothing like that. But it looks like that's the only option we've got. When we went north, we saw a jaguar, and the west seems too dense for us to tackle. Besides, if we follow the sun, we can't go far wrong…"

"So, we follow the sun. I like the sound of that, but where exactly are we going?"

"We need to find an elevation of some sort. No way would a plane see us from here. I'm hoping if we go east, we might find an elevation we can send a signal from. And besides," he added, "we need to find some water to drink and also to make sure we keep our wounds clean."

"Ain't no guarantee we're going to find that just because a book said so," Tess harrumphed.

"Well, sounds like a plan," Rachel said, smiling. "How soon do we get going?"

"As soon as we can fold these sleeping bags and get the rest of our gear together."

"Okay, let's do it, people," Craig said, spreading his arms. "We're going to conquer the jungle."

Rachel groaned as her stomach rumbled. She didn't feel ready to conquer anything.

They started packing.

*****

Brian snapped a twig and placed it in Rachel's hair. He was

57

trying to ignore the fact that he was smarting from the cut on his head.

"Hey," she protested.

"How're you doing, beautiful?" he asked with a grin.

"I'm fine. Just fine," she said, lightly rolling her eyes at him.

"That you are..." he winked.

She pretended to ignore him, but a corner of her mouth turned up in a smile.

They had walked for over two hours, and there was no elevation nor water in sight. And after thirty minutes of walking, they had tired of small talk. Craig held his injured arm with his other hand, intermittently. Rachel quickly got tired, but Tess was walking as if she had been born for this sort of thing, so Rachel decided not to complain but to bear it as manfully as she could.

The forest seemed silent; however, they could feel movement around them even though they could not hear it. There was no way the forest could ever be completely silent, Rachel thought. Although the scenery appeared picturesque, they found it very difficult trudging through the undergrowth.

Suddenly, before they could fully realize it, they came to a clearing. And then, in front of them was the most beautiful river they had ever seen. It looked so clear, so pure. The sun shimmered on its surface, making it look silvery. They eagerly walked towards it. Rachel absently opened the book she had placed in her backpack, just to see if it said anything about this 'water.'

The others all rushed forward and left her scanning the book. Curiously, the first page she opened read: "***Look closely into the water. Do not shrink from it. Then and only after all has been revealed can you cross it***."

Rachel stared at the words, not comprehending. She shrugged and went on after the others. But she wondered why the others were stopping in their tracks by the river's edge. She glanced into the river. *What on earth?!*

It was impossible, but there she was. In the water was her reflection. Or was it? She could see herself along with other people in the water. But her face kept changing. It was surreal.

Here was the time when she was seven years old, the first time she could ever remember telling lies to her mother. She had stolen some change from her mother's purse to buy candy. She had lied about it, but her mother later found out, and she was spanked. And yes, here was the time she sneaked out of school with her friend, Karen. It couldn't be.

Her whole life was playing out before her eyes. Every bad thing she had ever done, every unkind word she had ever uttered was showing right before her very eyes. She could not comprehend it and stood there rooted to the spot. She wanted to turn away, but she couldn't.

After each scene, the river seemed to become muddier and dirtier with each crime committed. She could feel the others standing beside her, but none of them moved. Then she heard a cry; Tess' voice.

"I can't take this anymore! This is crazy. We must have been drugged!"

With that, she stepped away from the river's edge and began to walk away. Rachel wanted to call her back, but her throat had closed. Neither could she go after her because she couldn't move from the spot. She felt an overwhelming sense of remorse.

The tears began to fall off her face as she saw every bad deed she had ever done, and then she began to sob harsh ragged sobs. She knelt at the water's edge. She couldn't explain what was happening to her. But she kept saying, "Oh, God, I'm sorry, I'm sorry." She repeated it over and over.

Beside her, she could hear Craig and Brian doing the same. After a while, when she wondered if the images would ever stop and if the river could get any dirtier, they stopped. But the feeling of remorse still gripped her. She had been horrible, and even now, she had lied to her mother. She wept with shame.

After a while, she began to calm down. The sobs became less ragged, and she could lift her head from the river's edge. She turned to face Craig and Brian. They both had streaming faces.

"What happened?" she asked Brian hoarsely.

He wiped his face. "I don't exactly know. But I saw some things on the river, and though they were all about me, they weren't exactly pretty," he said in a broken voice.

"It was the strangest thing," Craig admitted. "Things I had forgotten, things I was so thoroughly ashamed of, right before my eyes."

"It was the same with me! They were all about me," Rachel added. "But I don't know how we all saw these things at the same time. It doesn't make any sense."

"It's really weird. But one thing's for sure, this jungle is no ordinary place," Brian surmised.

"Where the hell is Tess?" Craig asked no one in particular.

"I think she moved away. Bet she couldn't take what she saw," Rachel said and immediately shrank at the disapproving glare from Craig.

"Let me go look for her," he said and got up. Brian and Rachel stared at each other.

"Brian, what do you think is going on?" Rachel asked, searching his face as if for clues.

"I have no idea. This place is much more than just a jungle."

"So, what do we do now?"

"I don't know. There doesn't seem to be any way around this place except to cross the river."

"You mean swim?"

"No, we won't have to do that." He pointed to some rocks in the river. The river's color had changed from sparking crystal to deep muddy brown. "We can step over that to the other side." He pointed far off into the distance. "Can't be too sure but looks like there's a hill of some sort over there."

"Yeah, that's what the book said," Rachel voiced, her fore-head creasing.

"What book said what?" Brian asked, confused.

"The book said we should cross the river, but only after all has been revealed or something like that," Rachel said while struggling to retrieve the book from her backpack.

"What has been revealed? I don't understand."

"I guess it means what we saw..." Rachel scanned the pages for the instructions.

"Where is it?" Brian asked. "Show me."

"That's just the problem. I can't seem to find it," she muttered, puzzled.

"Let me," Brian said and took the book from her. He scanned the whole book, but apart from the instruction on the front cover, he could find no other sentences within.

"I can't believe it. It was right here," Rachel balked, taking it from him to search again.

Craig and Tess interrupted them.

"Well, what do we do now?" Craig asked, trying to smile. It was clear he was not yet himself. He wondered if he would ever be. The things he had seen were nothing to smile about.

"We cross the river," Brian said, pointing to the rocks.

Craig cupped his hands to his eyes and squinted. "Looks like we might find our hill there."

"What? Cross this river?" Tess gasped, her pale face unable to conceal her fear. "No way am I going to even look at this river. There's something wrong with it."

"We all saw it, Tess. Besides, you never know; it might do you some good," Brian encouraged.

"Look, let's just get a move on, okay? This place gives me the creeps." Tess would never tell the others what she saw in the river. She didn't want to be reminded of how cruelly she had treated her mother and brother. The river was making her out to be something she was not - a monster. And she refused to believe it.

"Okay, we'll go across one at a time," Brian directed. "Craig, you go first."

Craig rolled up his trousers and crossed safely to the other side.

"Tess, you go next..."

"I'm not ready," she murmured. "Let Rachel go."

Rachel remembered something. "Yeah, the book said we can't cross it until all has been revealed." Brian gave her a look that said '*it's got to be written in invisible ink!*' She ignored him. "I think you need to look into the water, Tess." She wanted to add, "And see yourself as you truly are..." but didn't.

Tess sneered. "The book, the book... What book? That was what got us into trouble in the first place; you and your precious book!"

"Tess, stop talking like that. Now, will you cross, or should other people go before?" Brian hissed.

"You all cross. I'll go last," Tess said defiantly.

Rachel crossed. Brian tried again to cajole Tess to cross, but she refused. So, he crossed too. Then they all watched Tess as she crossed.

She took one tentative step at a time, trying to look at the stones alone and not at the water. But when she was climbing the third stone, she tripped and fell in.

"No!" Craig cried. "Swim, Tess! Swim," he instructed.

Tess began to swim with broad, powerful strokes. The three of them could see the fear in her eyes, and that fear made her move faster. The scene that followed would be indelibly etched in their minds forever.

Out of the river, a creature bobbed and began to move towards Tess with surprising speed. Rachel let out a scream. Craig and Brian shouted, "Tess, look out!" But they were seconds too late.

Tess was soon swallowed up in the gaping jaws of a crocodile. Rachel shrank in horror at what she had witnessed. It couldn't be. The creature disappeared down the river as quickly as it had appeared, with a sickening crunch. Craig crouched at the river's edge, his mouth hung open. Brian covered his eyes.

"Tess!" Craig began to scream, his voice agonized. There was no answer. "Tess!" he screamed again and again, the cry echoing all around the jungle.

Brian kept shaking his head and biting his lip as the tears fell. His mind couldn't comprehend what he had just seen. Rachel retched then curled into a fetal position and began to weep.

9

Chapter 9

"Do you think they just forgot to call, honey?" Donna said when they got up the next morning. Her eyes were heavy. She had not slept well the previous night. The journey to Brazil was supposed to take several hours, but it was over twenty-four hours now, and they had heard nothing from the kids. Donna was more than a little agitated, especially since they couldn't reach them on their cell phones.

"I'm sure they'll call, honey," Kevin said with a confidence he did not fully feel. "You know how kids are. Maybe they could not charge their phones."

Not Brian, Donna thought. He always did the responsible thing. He would have found a way to get in touch, she thought but kept it to herself.

"Well, I'll have to be off to work now," Kevin said, giving her a peck on the cheek. "Call me when Brian gets in touch."

Donna watched him go, feeling strangely bereft.

*****

Sierra woke up that morning to the sound of her alarm and

got out of bed rather angrily and unsure why. Then it hit her. Rachel! That daughter of hers hadn't called her yet.

She tried Rachel's cell again, but it was switched off. *Humph*, she thought, not surprised. It was just like Rachel to forget to charge her phone. Too bad Rachel hadn't given her any of the teachers' numbers who were to accompany them on the trip so she could call them. She really should have insisted on it.

Come to think of it, it was rather odd that the school was planning a geography trip during the holidays. But the letter had been clear, and she had no reason to doubt its veracity. So, she got up to prepare for work and decided she would try Rachel's phone again later.

*****

"Any word from your brother yet?" Mrs. Patricia Daniels asked her daughter, Sally, as she wiped her hands on her apron. She leaned against the counter and wiped the sweat off her sleeve.

Thankfully, the lunch crowd had finally eased, and she could have some breathing space. Running a restaurant sapped all her energy, but Sally was such a gift to her. Now, at twenty-one, Sally had decided she was going to help run the family business.

"Craig?" Sally said, laughing and tossing her long hair as she dried the dishes. "Don't expect it, Mom. I'm sure he's already forgotten all about us."

"How can you say that?" Patricia remonstrated.

"Mom, you know your son. He'll be so excited and so busy enjoying himself, he'll hardly be able to spare a thought for us."

"He could at least have called," the older woman grumbled.

"Oh, I guess he'll come around to it soon. Maybe I could prompt him, though," Sally said, fishing around in her pocket for her cell phone. "I hope this won't be horribly expensive," she said as she dialed Craig's number. She listened for a few seconds and dialed again. But it was still switched off. "Sorry, Mom. Can't get through. Craig must have forgotten to charge his phone. It's switched off."

"That boy!" Patricia remarked. "When is he ever going to grow up?"

"Hopefully soon, Mom. Sooner than we both expect. Maybe even after this trip," Sally said lightly.

Patricia grunted but said nothing. The sound of the restaurant doors opening reminded them that they had a business to run, and they returned to their tasks.

*****

Mary finished her last class and was out as soon as the bell rang. She waved and smiled at her second graders as they filed out of the classroom, even though her heart was breaking. Her daughter was like these smiling cherub-faced children once. Where had she gone wrong?

Tess had started running away from home since she was thirteen, not long after her father died. Wherever there was trouble, Tess found it. She had been in and out of different schools, in and out of juvenile detention, and sentenced with community service a couple of times, but nothing seemed to change Tess. And now, she had run off again, leaving only a note that said nothing.

Mary felt nothing but pain. It was painful that with all the discipline she had tried to instill, all the counseling, all the love she had showered on her daughter, and all the anxious nights she had spent worrying about when she would come home, Tess appeared to have no regard for her family and her future.

She felt like giving up. She could not cope with the pain and grief anymore. She decided that, for her own sake and Francis' sake, she would stop giving herself so much heartache over Tess. There was only so much a mother could do, and hopefully, when Tess was tired of running, she would come home to roost.

*****

"Do you still think we should go?" Donna asked hesitantly as she sat by her dressing table, staring dismally into the mirror.

Kevin adjusted his bow tie and leaned over to kiss his wife. "It beats sitting by the phone," he said, smiling, even though he too was worried. "Besides, Donna, you did so much work to put the benefit together. Think of all the people that'll be there. Think about all the people you could help with the money raised from this concert."

"I know, Kev, but–"

"The kids will be fine, Donna. I'm sure by the time we get back, we'll have heard from them. Tonight is your night, darling. I'm so proud of you. You deserve to be honored and appreciated."

Donna smiled a tremulous smile and took his hand, her heart brimming over with love for the man who stood beside her. She was so glad that after their business investments had made them millions, and she had told him that she wanted to leave the law firm where she was working and establish a charitable foundation, he had agreed.

Her heart was so full of love for him when they danced together at the benefit. And when she saw how much money they had raised from the concert, she felt like it would burst. Only one thing clouded that night. And that was the fact that they found no messages on their answering machine when they got home.

10

Chapter 10

Brian didn't know how long they sat by the river's edge, but he felt they had been there long enough. Nightfall wasn't far off. The heat was stifling in the wet, warm forest. Rachel was scared speechless. She couldn't say a word. Brian wondered how he got the dumb idea to fly to any place anyway.

Craig kept moaning, "What am I going to tell her mother?" He felt so guilty for bringing her on the trip and began to rue the day he had agreed to travel with Brian.

Brian knew they had to go on, hard as that seemed. There were so many ways to die in the jungle, he thought, and none of them were pleasant. As usual, he took the lead.

"Guys, we have to get going," he told them. Neither of them stirred. He knew they needed to get water and food soon. The river seemed clear but after what happened to Tess he could not bring himself to suggest they drink it. He figured they could get some tropical bananas if they looked hard enough, and they could find a stream somewhere. He wasn't ready to give up yet. He shook Craig, who looked like a shell of himself. "Craig, you've got to get up. You've got to stay alive. Tess would have wanted that."

"Shut up, Brian," Craig said, his eyes red and puffy. "You don't know what the hell Tess would have wanted. None of us knew. I don't know what she would have wanted. I hardly knew anything about her. All I wanted was a girl that would make me feel good about myself. I wasn't even interested in her as a person."

He had never felt more sober in his life. He had taken a good hard look at himself, and he was unhappy with what he saw.

Brian pulled him to his feet. "We've got to get moving." He lifted Rachel and pulled her chin up. "Rachel, look at me," he pleaded.

She was looking everywhere else except at him. He shook her. She focused on his face.

"Hey, the wound on your head's not there anymore," she said, puzzled.

"What are you talking about?" Brian asked and then touched his forehead, which now felt smooth.

Rachel glanced at her ankle and couldn't find the bruise that was there earlier.

Craig rubbed his arm, and it was smooth with no sign of any injury. "What is this place?" he wondered aloud.

"This is no ordinary jungle," Rachel muttered, nervously.

Brian had no idea what was happening, but he felt they didn't have time to ponder.

"Look at me," he insisted. "We have to get out of here. True, we've seen some terrible things out here today, but I know we can get through this. We have to get through this." He kissed her forehead. "I love you."

Unwillingly, she got to her feet, and the three of them began to trudge away from the river. A mile away from the river, Brian found a bunch of bananas, but his two companions were hardly interested in eating, even though they were starving. Craig was still torn up over Tess, and Rachel couldn't get over the horror of it. They drank water from a stream that appeared to be an offshoot of the river. They walked for an hour before they came to a sort of elevation. It was a small grassy hill that looked high enough for a low-flying helicopter to spot.

Finally, Brian thought. This was where they would be rescued. Craig and Brian looked for bamboo and erected a shelter. Yes, things were looking up, Brian thought, even though Rachel was yet to speak and Craig hardly uttered more than a syllable.

They lit a fire that night, using sticks, stones, and some rotting bark that had fallen off a tree. Brian did most of the work himself, glad that his survival training had come to good use. He tried not to think of what he had seen on the river that afternoon. They would surely be rescued soon, he thought. What happened to Tess was horrible, but hopefully, the rest of them would be able to leave this place in one piece.

He sighed as they settled down to sleep. Things would look better in the morning.

*****

Dawn couldn't come fast enough. Their second morning in the jungle. Rachel stirred beside Brian, and he stroked her hair. Craig got up and folded his sleeping bag. His eyes were red and puffy, and he didn't look like he had slept much.

He gave Brian a look that said, 'What now?' Brian shrugged. They would have to wait for a plane to fly overhead - or something - and then get on the hill and wave vigorously.

Rachel suddenly sprung up from sleep. She reached for

Brian's hand. "Brian," she whispered in a hoarse voice. She looked like someone that had been dragged through hell and back.

"*Shh*," he whispered back and kissed her hair. "It's going to be okay. We're going to be rescued soon, I promise."

"Brian," she said with conviction. "We have to follow the book or else we won't get out of here. I had a dream..."

He kissed her on the lips. "You're just stressed out, darling; we all are."

"Brian, listen to me. I saw Tess last night in my dream. She was standing on one of the stones in the river, and she looked so...tortured. I called out to her and told her to come to the other side of the river, but she said it was too late. She had missed her chance because she refused to follow the book. She said she knew it was right all along, but she did not want to believe it because that would mean that she needed help to go on her journey, and she had always felt she could do it on her own. Before I could ask her what she meant, she disintegrated before my eyes.

"We can't just follow logic here. Surely, what we saw yesterday was proof of that. Tess didn't follow the book, and she got eaten."

Brian was exasperated. He ran his hands through his hair. "Look, you expect me to believe that some book is controlling what happens to us here? And what would be the sense of that?"

"I don't have all the answers, Brian, but trust me on this one. We can't stay here unless the book says so," she said, sitting up. "Besides, this hill is too small for any plane to see us, except it's a helicopter."

"My father will have people searching for us by now. They'll use a helicopter," Brian said confidently. "All we have to do is wait."

He pulled her to her feet. "Now, my darling, what would you like to eat? There's a bunch of bananas leftover from yesterday, and perhaps we can look around to see if there are other edible things in this jungle," he said in a light-hearted tone.

Rachel kept silent. She desperately wanted to believe that Brian was right, but she knew he was not.

They ate some bananas and drank a little water. Brian told her some funny stories to pass the time, but Rachel didn't feel like talking. She listened and tried to resist the urge to open the book and see what it said.

Craig seemed to be in a world of his own. He didn't say anything but just stared off into space.

She didn't know when it happened exactly, but the heat of the overhead sun, combined with their physical and emotional exhaustion, made them all fall fast asleep. They did not see the black boa constrictor slowly slithering up to them. Something made Rachel open her eyes. Perhaps it was the snake's soft hiss or the sensation of something crawling around, but she got up and began to scream in terror.

Soon, all three of them were surrounded by three monstrous looking snakes. The snakes began slithering up on their legs and arms. They got entangled in them. Rachel kept screaming as a snake tried to make its way around her neck.

She tried calling out to Brian and Craig, but both were struggling with snakes too. Her worst nightmare had finally come true. They should never have come to this hill.

In her desperation, she cried out: "God help us!"

There was no answer. No bolts of lightning, no thunder, no gentle breeze - nothing. But like magic, the snake slithered off her body. Then they slithered off Brian and Craig's arms and began to crawl away. They left as quickly as they had come.

The three of them stood motionless for what seemed like an eternity, watching the snakes, then they all began talking at once. They tried to ease the strain on their shoulders and necks.

"What was that?" Craig asked, incredulous.

Brian held Rachel by her shoulders. "What did you do? Are you alright?"

Craig checked himself for bites or injuries. Amazingly, there were none.

"God helped us, guys. He actually did. We asked him for help, and He helped us," Rachel said slowly, like she didn't believe it.

Brian was speechless for a moment, then he said, "Rachel, I don't know what the hell just happened, but I know we could have died. We've gotta get out of here. Those snakes might return."

"Where are we going?" Craig asked warily.

"We go where the book says we go," Rachel replied decisively.

"Well, it's awfully strange that you seem to be the only one who can read this book," Brian said, taking the book from her. He opened it and read: "***Go through the way of the miry clay, west of the hill. Do not struggle against it for you will surely be lifted out.***"

Brian closed the book, a frown of consternation on his face.

"Well, what does it say?" Rachel asked eagerly.

"I don't understand. It says something about miry clay, but we're to go west of the hill. Here, you read it," he said, giving her the book.

She opened the book and scanned its pages. The book was empty except for the first page. "I can't find anything," she said to Brian. "Show me."

Brian leaned over and scanned the pages again. "That's funny.

It was right here," he said.

Rachel's eyebrows knitted together. "You know, this is exactly what happened when we were at the river. The instructions I had just read disappeared after I read them. Perhaps that's how this book works. The instructions come only when we need them."

"This is the weirdest thing I've ever seen," Brian murmured.

"So, tell me exactly what the book said," Rachel asked, her gaze intent.

He took a deep breath and said, "It said to go through the way of the miry clay that lies west of the hill and not to struggle against it because we will be lifted out, whatever that means."

Rachel shook her head. "I guess we'll know when we get there. I think we should start heading there right away."

Craig, who had been quiet all along, suddenly chipped in. "What, are you guys nuts? Can't you see? This whole thing is sick. The book keeps getting us into trouble, and you want to keep doing what it says?" He wondered why it had taken him so long to realize it. The book actually killed Tess. If they had not followed it, perhaps she would still be alive.

"No, Craig. It keeps getting us out of trouble, and the only way we're going to stay out of trouble is to follow it," Rachel retorted.

Craig shook his head. "Being in the jungle for two days has fried your brain. Listen to yourself. Our only way to be rescued is to stay on top of this hill and let a plane come rescue us," Craig said.

Brian turned to him. "But look here what just happened. There were snakes right here, they almost had us, man. We could have been killed."

"It was so awful," Rachel shuddered. " But I think if we follow the book it will help us get out of here."

"And you expect me to believe that? That's rich, that's really rich," Craig snorted.

"So, you're not coming with us?" Brian asked in concern.

"Not a chance."

"Craig, think about it…"

"Don't tell me to think about it," Craig said, shouting, pushing at Brian's chest. "This is all your fault. If you had not come up with this crazy idea to travel to Brazil, then we wouldn't be here right now." He turned to Rachel. "And if it wasn't for you and your precious book, Tess would still be alive too."

He had decided not to hold back. Perhaps it would make them listen to reason.

"Craig!" they both cried.

"Look, just leave me alone, both of you. You can go off and die on your own; I'm staying put here. When I get rescued, I'll tell them to look for you."

For the first time, he felt he was the level-headed one. He hoped they would find their way back to the hill, but if not, he would help the rescue party look for them.

Brian lunged at Craig in desperation. He would force Craig to go with them, whatever it took, he thought, but Rachel held him back.

"That won't help anything. Remember what we saw on the river. Don't do something you'll regret later."

Brian grunted and turned away from her. Rachel went to Craig. "Craig, I don't know exactly who's to blame for this mess, but the fact is we have to get out of here, and the book is the only way out. Trust me; we're not dealing with ordinary stuff here. Remember how our wounds miraculously disappeared? This is way beyond what we can imagine," she said softly.

Craig gave her a desultory look. "You see, that's your problem. Your imagination. It's certainly hyperactive."

"But you saw the stuff on the river yourself!" she protested. He did not look at her.

"Does this mean you're not coming with us?" she asked.

"Go away, Rachel," he said coldly.

"Let's go," she said, turning to Brian.

They made their way slowly down the hill, both wondering if they were doing the right thing. Brian felt like screaming at Craig, but he knew his friend's mind was made up. His only reassurance was that Craig knew how to take care of himself in the jungle.

Craig didn't even give them a farewell glance.

11

Chapter 11

S ierra knew something was fishy when she tried Rachel's number again the next morning and it was still switched off. She began to feel a little uneasy. She then called the school and asked for information concerning the students' school trip to Wyoming but was informed that there was no such thing, and the school was not aware of any trip. Sierra saw red.

Had Rachel lied and tried to make a fool out of her? After all she had done for her?! That girl was so ungrateful!

She called some of Rachel's friends in quick succession; Tiffany, Darla, and Rose, but they seemed to have no idea about Rachel's trip. She then stormed into her daughter's room, searching for clues, anything that would give her a hint as to where her daughter might have gone. The drawers did not reveal anything, but after searching carefully by Rachel's bedside, she found a poem addressed to her daughter and signed 'Brian Anderson.' The gall of the girl, she thought to herself bitterly.

How many times had she told Rachel that there were not to be any boyfriends? Instinctively, she knew Rachel was with him.

She searched for the name in the phone book and felt reasonably convinced that she had found them. Never mind that she would be late for work. She was going to pay them a surprise visit, bring her daughter home with her, and then ground her for at least a year.

*****

"I'm starving," Rachel muttered, moments after they got to the bottom of the hill. She didn't want to think about them leaving Craig behind or the horrible things that had happened. She wanted to put them all behind her, but at the same time she was terrified of what might happen next while they were still in the jungle. "Can we please look for something to eat?"

"Well, I'm glad your appetite's improved now. You didn't want to eat anything not too long ago," Brian said dryly.

"Battling those snakes has worked up my appetite," Rachel said grimly.

They continued walking until they found some bananas, and then Brian cut some off.

"I hope we won't have to live only on bananas," Rachel said as he handed her some.

"I'm sure there are lots of things we could try, but we've just got to find out what is edible and what isn't," Brian said as he peeled a banana.

"I wish I could have a bath. I feel so filthy," Rachel said in disgust as she lifted her left arm to smell her armpit.

"Well, you still look delectable to me," Brian said. "But perhaps we could wash a little if we find a spring. I saw one around here before we went up the hill."

He found the spring again and after filling their bottles with water, Rachel splashed water on her face. She longed to pour water over her body, but that would be impossible unless...

"Brian, would you excuse me for a minute? I really need to..."

"Shower?" Brian finished for her. She nodded. "Sure, but how long will you need?"

"About an hour," she teased. "No, really, I'll be done in fifteen."

Brian pursed his lips. "Fifteen minutes is too long for you to stay alone on your own. There are lots of creatures and critters moving around. If I left, even if it was just for a few minutes, you might not be able to defend yourself."

Rachel's face fell. She so wanted to cleanse herself from all the dust and grime on her body, but she knew Brian was right. Brian's face took on a conspiratorial look.

"Tell you what, I'll stand right there," he said, pointing to a spot not far away from her but out of sight. "And I'll turn my back and be on the lookout for dangerous creatures while you can have your leisurely soak."

Rachel looked uncertain. The plan had some flaws. "Promise you won't peek?"

He put a hand over his heart. "Promise."

"Not even a little..." she teased, smiling.

"Well, maybe just a little," he said with a wink.

"Brian!" she protested.

"I was just kidding," he said. "In fact, I'm going to start my duty right now." And giving her a mock salute, he walked to the designated spot away from her and turned his back.

She hesitated a little then gingerly removed her clothes and stepped under the spring. After a few minutes, Brian slowly turned around to observe what Rachel was doing. He let out a soft whistle as he watched her. He definitely liked what he saw.

Rachel stepped out from under the spring feeling refreshed.

She wore her clothes and went to meet Brian, who was still standing with his back towards her.

"Well, my knight," she said while rubbing his head affectionately. "You certainly did a very good job of watching over me."

You don't know how well, Brian thought with a smile.

"Now, it's your turn to have a wash."

Brian gave her a mock groan. "Aw, mom, do I have to?"

Rachel returned a stern look. "Or do I have to make you?"

"Go ahead, sweetheart," he said, giving her a once over.

"Brian, you're a naughty boy!" she cried.

"It's one of the reasons you love me," he said with a wink and headed for the spring. Rachel shook her head and turned her back. The quicker they got themselves cleaned up, the better.

Soon, they were trudging on again in the jungle, trying to get west of the hill. They bantered and joked and seemed carefree. It was as if they had forgotten that they were lost in the jungle. They seemed lighthearted, but there was something more in the air. Rachel didn't know what it was, but Brian had an inkling.

They found some oranges and more bananas. Brian peeled the oranges with his pocket knife.

"This jungle is going to make vegetarians out of us," Rachel said when they stopped to eat.

"You know, I could die for a hot steak right now," he said longingly.

"We've been walking all day, and we still don't see anything that looks remotely like clay or something," Rachel grumbled. "Are you sure we're going west?"

"Sure we are. I know my geography," he said indignantly. "But Rache," he added softly, "do you really think we've got to follow this book? It looks like we're just going deeper into the jungle."

"Just trust me on this one, Brian. Didn't your mom ever tell you to trust a woman's instincts?"

"Many times," he grinned.

"Then let's go on," she said, pulling him to his feet.

They kept walking. Brian couldn't help scanning the skies overhead. Surely, they must be looking for them.

*****

Kevin chewed on his Cuban cigar and downed another Martini, but nothing could relieve the restlessness he felt. Where on earth was his son?! He glanced over at Donna, who was pacing in the living room.

He felt like a fool, but his pride would not allow him to say how he felt. They'd had an ugly scene with Rachel's mother, who was threatening to sue them for kidnapping her daughter. It had been hard to convince her that they didn't know Brian hadn't told the truth about the trip.

Donna was very upset. The situation wasn't helped by the frantic calls from Brian's grandparents and extended family.

Kevin felt betrayed by his son. He had trusted him. Had Brian run off somewhere else? Or had something happened to him and his friends?

They had contacted the police, and they had other people at Interpol searching for them at this very moment. His many contacts came in handy, and the police had assured him they would be found. Kevin knew Donna was resisting the urge to say, "I told you so." But she had been right on this one. He just hoped they found them soon. He would never let Brian out of his sight again.

The phone rang, and Donna practically flew to pick it. "Yes,

Mrs. Anderson speaking," she said softly, trying hard not to sound hysterical.

She listened for a few minutes and said, "Thanks so much, we'll be by the phone." Then quietly, she placed the receiver in its cradle.

She turned to face Kevin. "They think they found something," she said with tears in her eyes.

*****

"Mom!" Francis called out as he dropped his bag on the sofa. He could smell something baking. With any luck, his mother would be making some cookies. He couldn't wait to taste them.

"How was school today?" Mary replied as he sauntered into the kitchen.

"Cool," he said, trying to peek at what was in the oven.

His mother smiled at him. "It's your favorite, chocolate chip cookies."

Francis resisted the urge to shout 'Yippee.' After all, he wasn't a little kid anymore; he was almost sixteen. Instead, he said sedately, "Cool."

He sat down on a chair in the kitchen and asked his mom, "Any word from Tess yet?"

"No, she hasn't called," she replied, frowning.

"I wonder what she's doing right now..." Francis said wistfully.

"I guess she's doing what she always does. Getting into all kinds of trouble and not caring that we're worried sick about her," Mary said vehemently. She couldn't hide how fed up she was with her daughter's behavior.

"I wish Dad were here," Francis muttered involuntarily.

Mary ignored his statement and turned her back to him. He

could tell from the muffled sounds she made that she was crying.

"Mom, I'm sorry," he said and got up to give her a hug.

Mary turned her red eyes to him. "It's not your fault, Francis. I know your dad would have been better with Tess. I'm just... I'm such a terrible parent," she sobbed.

"Oh, Mom, don't say that..." Francis said reproachfully. It was at times like this that he thought he hated his sister. She was so hard to figure out. Why was she so...so restless?

Tess had been a constant source of anxiety ever since their father died eight years ago. She had been arrested twice for petty theft and for having drugs in her possession. She had run away from home countless times.

Francis was confused about why she would want to leave them because he adored his sister. It was true she had a sharp tongue, and he hated being the butt of her cruel remarks, but she was very protective of him, and she could be fun to be with at times. She was also very knowledgeable on what was cool and what wasn't. But he really wished she had more practical knowledge of human relations.

"Mom, don't worry," he said, patting his mother's shoulder. "It's going to be alright. It will. I promise," he added, trying to sound reassuring as he held her. But he wasn't sure things were going to be alright or if they would ever be.

12

Chapter 12

"I don't think I can walk any further," Rachel grunted, collapsing into a heap on the ground.

Brian plunked down beside her. "It's about time we stopped anyway. It's getting dark, and my flashlight's batteries are going out."

"Do you think we can light a fire?"

"Not too sure about that. I'm not sure we can get any wood around here."

"Oh, well..." Rachel muttered, lying down. "I think I'll just try to make myself comfortable."

Brian lay down beside her. Neither of them spoke for a while, as they were both thinking about Craig and wondering what had happened to him. But it seemed like there was an unspoken agreement between them not to mention his name.

Soon, Rachel began to shudder. The air was chilly, and she wished they could get some sort of heat. Brian placed his arms around her to warm her. Still, she shuddered.

"I know how we can get warm," he whispered softly in her ear.

"Really? How?"

He fished around in his back pocket, his hand gripping something.

"Say, what do you have there? Your old granny's quilt?" she teased.

He smiled. "Even better."

Before she could question him further, his mouth enveloped hers in a hot, searing kiss, and she could feel the temperature rising by degrees. Brian had never kissed her like this before. She didn't realize what he was doing when he slowly took off her coat, nor did she fully understand what was happening when he removed his shirt. But when he began to press his body against hers, the heat became unbearable, and she knew that she could get burned.

She struggled against him. "Brian, stop!" she managed to let out.

But he wasn't listening. His hormones had defeated him. He was struggling to unbutton her blouse when she slapped him hard across the face. He got off her like lightning.

"What did you think you were doing?" she asked, eyes blazing.

Brian dragged a breath. This wasn't the way he had planned it, but the sight of her at the spring that evening...

"I'm sorry..." he managed hoarsely.

Rachel didn't want to look at him; one look and her resolve might just weaken, and she could risk getting burned. After all, she did love him, but she instinctively knew the book wouldn't approve of what he wanted.

"Let's just forget this happened, okay?" she said, looking anywhere else but at him.

"Okay," Brian muttered despondently, saddened at the

wasted opportunity.

Rachel faced him then. "Look, Brian. Remember what we saw on the river. We can't risk doing things we'll regret later."

"Fine."

"I love you," she whispered, willing him to believe it.

Brian turned over on his side and pretended not to hear. Rachel grew cold again, but this time, she knew it wasn't because of the weather.

*****

"It's been like three days; don't you think she should have called by now?" Mary said to her son as they sat down by the television a few hours later.

"I guess she would, but maybe she hasn't run out of money yet," Francis said cynically.

"You don't think anything has happened to her, do you?" she asked with apprehension in her voice.

"Nah," Francis said easily. "Tess can take care of herself. She always has."

Mary sighed. "I just wish we had an idea where she was."

Francis didn't answer. He was thinking much the same thing.

*****

They had switched places. Donna was sitting down with her hands folded over her laps while Kevin paced the room. He regretted being so indulgent and letting Brian travel on his own. Why hadn't he listened to Donna? He had been so thoughtless.

Thankfully, she was not blaming him. But still, it had been a long time since he last found himself in a situation he couldn't control, and now, the situation was getting to him. His money, influence, and power were proving worthless in the search for his son.

"Why won't they call?" Kevin wondered aloud, frustrated. It had been three hours since the first report came in, and they had heard nothing else. This whole business was stretching their nerves. He couldn't wait to see Brian and give him the verbal thrashing he deserved for putting them through this. And he would never let him fly the plane – ever again! Maybe he would even sell it.

As if hearing him, the phone rang.

Kevin went to pick it and listened quietly to the voice on the other end, his face expressionless. When he dropped the receiver, his face had taken an unearthly shade of gray.

"Yes?" his wife asked.

"They found three bodies in a car wreck, just a few miles away from the Rio de Janeiro airport. They were burnt beyond recognition, but they're trying to see if they could find some ID on them," Kevin said in a monotone. He could not allow himself to feel anything, or else he would break down completely.

Donna collapsed onto the couch, her mouth moving but no words coming out. Kevin turned his face away; the grief would surely tear his wife apart, and there was nothing he could do about it.

"But, why are there three bodies?" Donna asked in a high-pitched voice. "Four of them went on the trip..."

"I don't know. Maybe one of them got away or something," Kevin said in a broken voice.

"It's not them, Kev," she said with sudden conviction. "It's not their bodies."

Kevin wished he could agree with her, but he couldn't bring himself to say anything. If the kids were still alive, wouldn't they have heard from them by now? And their plane hadn't been found yet nor was it reported landing anywhere. They had simply vanished.

*****

The next afternoon, Patricia wiped her hands on her apron and sat down exhausted. It had been a long day, and the customers seemed to just keep coming and coming. Sally walked into the kitchen and sat down beside her mother.

"Are your feet killing you like mine are killing me?" Patricia asked, giving her daughter a tired smile.

Sally shook her head. "I thought they would never leave."

"Heard from Craig yet?" Patricia asked, wiping her hands on her apron.

"No. I guess they're too busy soaking up the sun in Brazil to bother about charging their phone batteries and talking to people like us," Sally said tiredly.

Patricia smiled. "It's a pity Brian's too young for you. You could have been with them right now."

"Aw, mom, I don't give a hoot about Craig's snotty friend or others like him," Sally said, wrinkling her nose in disgust.

"Oh, I wouldn't say Brian was snotty. He seems a decent enough guy," Patricia countered gently.

"Mom, you know what they always say about wolves in sheep's clothing... You can never tell," Sally said playfully.

"David's not a wolf, is he?" Patricia teased, referring to Sally's boyfriend.

"M-o-o-m!" Sally remonstrated, looking infuriated while her mother gave a little tinkling laugh. She always enjoyed seeing young people in love. It made her feel young again. She just wished Craig would be more like his sister. He was far too restless for her peace of mind.

Still, she wondered why he didn't call. But again, being thoughtful had never been one of Craig's virtues. Nor his dad's, she smiled to herself as she placed the dishes on the counter.

*****

Brian and Rachel awoke to the soft pitter-patter of rain falling on their faces. It was a slow, lazy drizzle at first, then it gathered intensity. They sought shelter under the trees, but it offered little protection from the relentless downpour.

"Can things get any worse?" Brian grumbled.

Rachel took a deep breath. "Brian, about yesterday…"

"Save it," he said, putting up a hand to silence her.

Rachel felt indignant. What was wrong with him? Wasn't she the one that was supposed to be angry?

The rain stopped as quickly as it had started, but they both felt wet and miserable. Without a word, Brian began marching in front. Rachel was tempted to rail at him for his childishness but held her temper in check. Two can play this game of silence, she thought. They began slogging their way through the jungle.

An hour passed, and they had not said a thing to each other. Rachel wondered if they would ever find the miry clay or if the instructions in the book had changed. She decided to take a quick peek at the book to see if she would find anything new. Brian was in front of her, and he didn't notice when she lagged to open the book. She was startled to read: "***As you go along in your journey, for as much as it is in your power, do your best to be at peace with your fellow travelers.***"

She closed it, indignant. Did this mean she had to apologize to Brian? She threw the book back into her backpack and marched after him. Sometimes, the book made no sense. No sense at all.

*****

Kevin dropped the receiver and looked at his wife.

"It's not them," he said flatly. He could not believe she had been right. Dared he hope?

"Thank God!" Donna cried, wiping the tears from her eyes.

"Well, maybe it's not them, but that doesn't mean they're not dead," Kevin said harshly. Better to always be prepared for the worst; he had learned that from his childhood.

"Kevin!" his wife cried in horror.

He turned to her in sudden anger. "Look, Donna. They can't find any trace of them. We have Interpol looking all over for them, and it's as if they disappeared from the surface of the earth. Don't you think if they were alive, they'd have called us by now?" he shouted.

He knew he was being unreasonable, but he couldn't help himself. The worst thing would be to have false hope and then realize that it was all for naught.

"Oh, Kev," Donna said, walking to him and placing a hand on his shoulder. "We can't give up hope. They'll come back; you'll see, they will."

Kevin raked a hand through his hair. "I just want this whole nightmare to be over," he muttered.

She stroked his hair. "Me too, Kev. Me too."

13

Chapter 13

Another hour and thirty minutes later, and it looked like they were no closer to the miry clay than when they first started, even though all the paths they had gone through were muddy due to the rain from earlier. They still had not said more than a few syllables in over three hours. Rachel was beginning to feel very uncomfortable. The words of the book etched indelibly on her mind. Suddenly, Brian stopped and gestured in front of them. They were standing in front of a swamp. There was no way to avoid it except to go back.

"This look like miry clay to you?" Brian asked cynically.

"I guess this has to be it," Rachel replied hesitantly.

"So, you think we should wade in?" Brian asked, raising his eyebrows.

"Yes... I mean, no. Wait," Rachel said, trying to collect her thoughts. "Before we go in Brian, there's something I want to say." She forced herself to look him in the eye. "I just want to say that I'm really sorry about last night, and though you'll thank me for it someday, I know I hurt you." She sighed. "I just want us to be friends again, you know?"

Brian looked at her for a long moment then turned away. A muscle worked in his jaw. "I'm sorry I acted like such a jerk," he said at last.

She came up behind him and put a hand on his shoulder. When he turned to look at her, she stretched out her hand. "Friends?"

"Friends," he said, grinning as he shook her hand.

Rachel gave herself a mental pat on the back. *There, that wasn't so hard.*

"Uh, Rache... I saw something yesterday," Brian began hesitantly.

"Really? What was it?"

"It was Craig."

Rachel put a hand to her mouth. "He wasn't dead, was he?"

"Ah, well, I'm not sure. You see, I saw him in my dream..."

Rachel gave him a quizzical look. "He seemed really frightened, Rache. He was looking so...how did you put it? He looked so tortured, and he told me that he wished he had followed the book. He looked rather ghastly. I tried to tell him that he could come with us, but he said that it was too late."

"It sounds so much like my own dream about Tess," Rachel said thoughtfully. "Do you think we should go look for him?"

"I don't know, Rache. As cold as this sounds, it's probably too late for him."

"Oh, Craig," Rachel muttered sadly, looking at the swamp. She gulped down sobs.

They stood there silently for a few minutes, each thinking about Craig and wondering why their holiday trip had gone so horribly wrong. Brian couldn't help but feel guilty about the whole thing because it had been his suggestion. But he was very angry as well.

He wasn't the first kid to go on holiday. Why did they have to go through this? What had they done to deserve this?

Rachel felt their experience was partly some retribution for lying to her mum. She knew her mother would be devastated and disappointed with her. But seriously, what had they done that was so awful? Couldn't they have enjoyed their getaway and come back to face the music, like so many other teenagers do? It really wasn't fair.

"So, what do you say? Do we jump in or not?" Brian asked, startling Rachel out of her reverie.

"Oh, this might be a mistake, but I don't think the book has been wrong so far. I don't think we really have any other option," she mused.

Brian rolled up his pant legs. "Ready?" he asked.

She finished rolling up her jeans. "Yeah."

Holding hands, they went together into the swamp. The swamp seemed to suck them right in. They couldn't move.

"Brian," Rachel cried. "Don't let go of me!"

"Rach, I don't really think this was a good idea," Brian said with fear in his eyes.

They tried moving forward, but for every step they took, the swamp seemed to push them two steps back. And it looked like they were beginning to sink too. They struggled in the mud for what felt like fifteen minutes, but they were getting nowhere. Rachel felt as if critters were crawling all over her body.

Brian searched for a tree branch, anything they could hold on to. But there was nothing. They began sinking deeper and deeper, and they couldn't hold on to each other anymore. Unwillingly, Brian had to let go of Rachel's hand. They had become submerged to trunk level in the swamp and were still sinking. Rachel remembered what happened with the snakes. They were in a desperate situation again.

"God, where are you? We need help, please save us!" she cried. But after a few minutes and they were still stuck fast, Rachel began to cry.

What if Brian had been wrong? She hadn't seen what the book said. What if they didn't make it out of there? Was she going to be buried alive in this swamp, after everything she has gone through? What if there was no power in the book and everything they had seen was just a hoax?

"Rachel," Brian shouted as they sank further and struggled to stay afloat.

"Yeah," she replied, her voice barely above a whisper. The swamp was getting to her waist, and she knew it would soon cover her neck.

"I have something I wanted to say too..."

"What is it, Brian?" she asked, looking into his fear-filled eyes.

"I just want to tell you how much I love you. Rachel Menendez, you're truly incredible. The way you talk, the way you smile, the way you laugh, your wisdom in everything has always blown my mind. I'm glad I've had the chance to get to know you. I love you so much, Rache. I really do."

Rachel beamed at him through her tears. She was too choked up with emotion to say anything.

"The way this looks, you might never get to know how much," he added sadly, glistening tears stroking his face.

Rachel thought about her family, her mom, her friends. She would miss them so much. All this wasn't fair, she thought. She still had a lot of things she wanted to achieve, places to visit, dreams to fulfill, but...

Wait a minute? They were following the book, weren't they? This wasn't part of the script.

"Brian, can you tell me exactly what the book said? I mean, repeat it word for word."

"But I've said it like a thousand times already…" Brian said, puzzled.

"Just tell me, Brian. This is important."

"Okay…" he muttered and furrowed his brows in concentration. "The book said: '*Go through the way of the miry clay; do not struggle against it for you will surely be lifted out.*'"

"Yes, that's it!" Rachel cried.

"What do you mean?" Brian asked, lost.

"Brian, stop kicking against the mud. Just let your body go limp. Like this," she said, demonstrating.

"Don't do that, Rachel! You want us to give up without a fight?"

"It's what the book said. We've got to believe in the book, the power in the book. We're not to struggle at all. It's like, you know, we're just to surrender and not try to do anything on our own. We will be pulled out."

"This is crazy," Brian said as he stopped kicking.

"Believe me, Brian. Everything the book says makes sense," Rachel said as the swamp continued to submerge them. It had reached the level of their necks and was about to cover their heads. "Don't worry, Brian. Just believe."

As the swamp covered their heads, all she could see was a sea of murky brown mud, and then everything went blank.

*****

Donna woke up suddenly and found Kevin still pacing. She didn't know when she'd dozed off on the sofa.

"Nothing yet?" she asked.

Kevin shook his head. Surely, they should have heard more

by now.

"We can hope," Donna muttered. "And pray," she added a bit more loudly. It was the one hope she had.

"Pray? Yeah, a lot of good that would do," Kevin remarked with a grimace.

"Look, Kevin, I know we've never really believed in God our entire adult lives, but if we ever needed Him, it's now."

"Go on, Donna, pray. I won't stop you. I guess praying makes *some* people feel better, and that's a good thing. As for me, I'm far too tense to do any kind of talking with the 'Almighty' right now," Kevin replied slowly as he continued pacing. Belief in the efficacy of prayer was a hope that he felt he could not afford.

Donna sighed. She had no idea how to start. She had been hoping someone could tell her but not even Kevin had an idea. She sat on the sofa with her hands on her lap, then she closed her eyes and began silently.

"Dear God..."

*****

Rachel bobbed to the surface gasping for air, in the cool, clear water. Her first thought was that she was alone. That was not good.

"Brian!" she cried, swimming around, searching for him.

He bobbed to the surface, shaking off water from his hair. "Rachel," he shouted, swimming towards her. They stared at each other as though they were not sure the other was real...

"I don't understand," Brian said, bewildered. "What happened?"

"I have no idea," Rachel said. "But I do think we should get out of here."

Brian looked towards the shore a quarter of a mile away.

"Good idea," he said, as they began to swim towards it.

They came out of the water slowly, panting and trying to take stock of their surroundings.

"Where are we?" Brian asked as he stepped out of the water and sat down on the grass. It certainly didn't look like the jungle they knew.

Rachel blinked and couldn't answer. The place was breath-takingly beautiful. The grass seemed like it had been freshly mowed, and flowers dotted the landscape. There were a few trees, but there was no dense foliage like they had seen before.

The sun was not hot but warm, caressing their bodies. Could they be in a park of some kind?

"Do you think we've died and gone to heaven?" Brian asked, puzzled.

Rachel smiled. "That's one way to explain it, but I don't know how we can tell for sure."

"This is amazing. The last thing I remember was being in the swamp, and now, I'm in this picturesque place. I feel like Alice in Wonderland or something," Brian said, unable to keep the awe out of his voice.

"I bet the book can tell us something," Rachel said, shaking off her waterproof backpack and opening it to extract the book. She eagerly scanned through the pages, but there was nothing. She was puzzled. She leafed through the pages again, one by one, but the book was empty.

"What did you find?" Brian asked, bending over her. He took the book from her and searched for himself, but the only page with something on it was the first page, as usual.

"That's strange," he said, stroking his chin.

"Everything about this whole experience has been strange," Rachel said, getting on her feet. "Come on," she said to Brian.

"Where are you going?" he asked as she began to walk away.

"To explore the land, of course. Come on!"

Brian slowly got to his feet, feeling as excited as Rachel apparently was to explore this strange new land.

"Look," she said, pointing excitedly. "Apple trees!"

Brian grinned in delight. *Now for some real fruit.* Apples were the only fruit whose taste he could tolerate. "Alright," he cheered.

They plucked a few apples and shared them equally. Brian finished his before Rachel and tried to persuade her to give him her last. When she adamantly refused, he tried to grab it from her, but she pulled it away from him and began to run.

Without missing a beat, he chased after her. She ran in circles, teasing him. And as her red hair blew in the warm breeze, he felt something stirring deep within his breast. He felt a lump in his throat and swallowed. Rachel was so beautiful.

"Gotcha!" he said when he suddenly pounced on her and they tumbled down in the grass. Their faces were close, inches away from each other, and he couldn't resist. He kissed her on the cheek softly.

Their eyes met, and hers seemed washed with unshed tears. There was a poignant silence until Rachel smiled, got up, and said, "Well, come along. Let's see what else we can discover."

Brian followed her, the strange unfamiliar fluttering deep within his breast. He was discovering a lot of things already, and the more he discovered, the more he felt like discovering. Would he ever finish discovering all there was to Rachel? He hoped not.

The area seemed peaceful. No wild animals were around, as far as he could see. There were no animal tracks nor anything to hint that wild beasts lived nearby.

They found some pears and ate them. He picked a bouquet of flowers for Rachel and felt her pleasure when she sniffed them and pronounced them beautiful, with an appreciative smile. A tendril of hair wafted across her face in the gentle breeze. He stared at her again and again.

While Brian was making his discoveries, Rachel was making discoveries every bit as important or even more so. Every blade of grass, every flower, and every tree she saw seemed to tell her something; that contrary to all her Biology teacher had said, there was a Creator. And all He created was good. Good, great, and wonderful. Absolutely marvelous.

A joy rose deep within her chest, one that she couldn't explain. It felt like...she had read it somewhere... "*All's well with the world; God is in His heaven.*"

She wondered what God was doing right now. Was He looking down at her, watching her and Brian walking through these woods together? Rachel stopped suddenly and caught herself. What was she thinking? She had never had time to think about God, much less what He was doing. But this journey had made her realize how real He was, and how near too. She wondered what Brian made of all this.

"Brian," she said with a wistful smile. "Don't you think God is just wonderful?"

"Yep," he said noncommittally.

She wasn't daunted. "Look at everything around us; the flowers, the trees, even the view. It's just breathtaking."

"Not as breathtaking as you..." he muttered, stars in his eyes.

Rachel lowered hers. Why was Brian talking like this all of a sudden, and why did she feel like her stomach was tied up in knots? It felt strange.

She tried to change the subject. "Look, Brian. Doesn't all this stuff make you think about God?"

"What do you mean?" Brian asked, unsure.

"God just seems so real. You know, like if I stretched my hand out far enough, I could just touch Him," she said, looking up at the sky.

"I'm not really sure I'd want to do that. I mean, wasn't it God that brought us to the jungle in the first place? We've almost been killed by jaguars and snakes, and we've had to pass through all kinds of things. And what about Tess and Craig? Didn't God just stand by and watch them die? I think God is someone we should be afraid of... You never know what He might do to you."

"Well, I don't understand how God works or why He does what He does, but I know that each time I called on Him, He always answered, one way or another, even when I didn't expect it."

Brian nodded and patted her hand. "It's been a very long day, and it's getting dark. We should be looking for a place to sleep now."

"Sure," she said, trying to hide her disappointment that Brian wasn't willing to discuss further.

They settled down under a grove of trees nearby, and Brian brought out the sleeping bag he'd been carrying in his backpack. Rachel still mused on whether God had intervened and could intervene in their lives while Brian struggled with resentment. If there was a God, then why didn't He save them from this mess, this never-ending journey? They didn't deserve the heartache they had been through.

Brian eventually settled into a fitful sleep, but Rachel stayed awake staring at the starlit sky.

14

Chapter 14

Kevin dropped the phone and put his head in his hands for a moment before turning to face his wife. She looked at him questioningly.

"They've called off the search," he said flatly.

"But why would they do that? They haven't found them yet," she said, bewildered.

"That, my dear, is exactly the point. It's been five days, five whole days, and there hasn't been any sign of them. They've been spending a lot of valuable manpower and resources looking for them, and they've only kept on because of me. They think the kids may have been kidnapped or more likely that they've run away and don't want to be found. The police said it's quite common among kids of their age group."

"But, but... They can't stop!" Donna said shrilly. "They just have to look harder, and then they'll find them. And our Brian wouldn't run away; he has no reason to."

"I'm sorry, darling," Kevin said, kissing her forehead, then he walked to the window to stare out into the distance. He forced himself not to think of anything. Despite the news, he suddenly realized that the loss of hope was not something he wanted to face. His lips shook as he was overcome with grief. "It seems like they'll just have to find their way back to us on their own..."

*****

Mary couldn't sleep. She couldn't shake off the feeling that something was wrong with Tess. She got up from her bed and went to Francis' room. He was sound asleep, and she stood by his bed, watching him. She wished with all her heart that Peter was still with them. It had been cruel to leave her with two teenagers. Why did he have to have cancer, of all things? And then he had lung cancer.

She had told him time and time again that he should quit smoking. But he never stopped until it was too late. Yet, she couldn't be angry with him. He was the nicest man she had ever known. Rather, she was angry with Tess for making her so worried.

She had been waiting for the phone to ring ever since she entered Tess' room and found the cryptic note: "Mother, I'm going away for a few days."

That had been all. No affectionate ending, no details of where she was going or with whom... She had just upped and left one morning before the rest of the house was up. Even if she wanted to search for Tess, she would have no idea where to begin. But she was getting agitated now.

Tess didn't have any money. So, she should have called by now to say that her money had run out. But she hadn't. And that could mean two things; either she was with someone who was taking care of her or she had got into some kind of trouble that was far too serious for her to call.

Mary sighed, turning away from Francis' sleeping form. She

crept wearily back to her room. She would not think the worst yet. She decided she would wait for another twenty-four hours, after which she was going to involve the police.

She lay down on her bed and waited for dawn to come.

*****

Rachel still couldn't sleep. The sound of crickets pierced through the stillness of the night, but that was not what kept her awake. She tried lying still so as not to disturb Brian, but her mind was too active to give her any sort of rest.

This whole journey had been incredible, right from the start. The crash, the book, the river, the snakes, Tess' death, and Craig's defection. She felt that all the elements of the journey combined to tell her something, but she had no clue what it was. Here they were in a wonderland, not knowing how they would get out, and now, the book was keeping silent, and Brian was acting so enchanted by her... What did it all mean?

She knew her mother would be wild with worry and grief, and she wished she could call and tell her she was alright. At least for now. But how long would their safety last?

*****

Sierra tossed around in bed, unable to sleep. She was being tormented by memories. Memories of when Rachel was a little girl, before her father left them. Memories of Rachel's first word, "Mama," and how her heart swelled when she heard it. Her wet, sweet kisses, her soft, rosy cheeks... Her wide smile that lit up her whole face. As if that wasn't enough, she was also tormented by memories of the lovely young lady her daughter had grown up to become. A beautiful young woman with just the right figure and heart-shaped face. Much like Sierra had looked when she was the same age... Rachel was very smart and wanted to become a lawyer, but now...nothing seemed certain anymore.

She remembered how grieved and disappointed she had been when she found out where her daughter had truly gone. After finding the note from Brian, her first thought was that Rachel had run off to get married. However, when she met the parents, they assured her that was not the case. Yet, no one could tell her if her daughter was alright. And those were the words she desperately needed to hear. It had been hard, working two jobs to support herself and her daughter, but she had felt it was worth it. Now, could it all have been for nothing?

At first, she had felt a terrible rage towards her daughter for betraying her. Running off with a boy was bad, but going to Brazil without telling her; that was pretty unforgivable. She had raised her daughter better than that.

Boys were to be avoided at all costs, at least until Rachel completed college, she had told her daughter again and again. They only wanted one thing, and when they were through, they tossed you into the bin for the next thing walking around in a skirt. She had told Rachel her own story a thousand times. Couldn't that girl listen to her mother?!

Perhaps, if Sierra had listened to her own mother, things would not have turned out so bad.

She had fallen in love with Luis Menendez at the tender age of fifteen. The first time she saw him, she had told herself he would be her husband someday. He was young, strong, and handsome, with good teeth. But he didn't even notice her. Not until she was seventeen.

Her mother told her he was no good, but she was too head over heels in love to listen. He was a mechanic, by then, and was earning good money, she thought. When she was eighteen, she got pregnant, then the dream wedding she'd envisioned got shifted forward. They had to have a quickie wedding in court. She had thought they would be happy together, but it turned out that, after a few months, nothing she did could please Luis. After a year, he ran off with another girl and had never bothered to look for them since then.

Sierra wanted to give Rachel the best, so she went back to school and took classes in Accounting, and she gave it her best shot. She got, not one job but, two good jobs and was proud of the fact that she was good at what she did. She hadn't allowed herself to be distracted by any other man. She felt their life was idyllic, but obviously, Rachel didn't think so.

She sighed for the umpteenth time and wondered if she hadn't been too harsh on her daughter. Had her demands that her daughter not date any guy until she finished college pushed her straight into Brian's arms?

It had been five days since they spoke. She wondered if she would ever have the answer to her question.

*****

Sally lay on her bed, too tired even to sleep. Her thoughts turned to Craig. She thought about her brother more than she cared to admit. She liked him for his carefree, happy-go-lucky ways and the charming effect he had on people. She even liked the way her friends always exclaimed, "Oh, is that your brother? He's so cute!"

She was quieter than he was, and she had always wished she had been a little more like him. She would definitely have had more friends.

What she didn't like about him was his irresponsibility. It was true she was the older sibling, but since their father died, he had promised that he would take on more in the family business. Their mother had to work so hard at the restaurant all day, and despite Sally's help, the work wasn't significantly lightened.

But Craig had always been too playful to be of serious help to the family business. He preferred hanging out with his friends to waiting tables. She didn't like waiting on tables so much herself, but then, what had to be done had to be done. She just wished he would grow up.

Sally felt it was partly her mother's fault that Craig was so irresponsible. Patricia over-indulged him and seldom scolded him, even when he did wrong, like not coming home all night after a party. Her mother would never let her get away with such behavior. Sally wasn't so sure if her mother would have agreed if she had been the one that wanted to go to Brazil.

Sally swallowed. She would no longer stomach Craig's juvenile behavior. It wasn't good for him or any of them. Whenever he returned from Brazil, something would have to be done about it. And if their mother refused to do anything, then she would.

15

Chapter 15

Brian yawned and stretched, then smiled at Rachel, who had been awake for some time and was staring pensively at the sky.

"So, where do we go today?" he asked, gesturing towards her backpack.

Obligingly, she pulled the book out and opened it. She flipped its pages before she announced: "Looks like we're still stuck here."

Brian fell back on the sleeping bag, his sandy brown hair tousled by sleep. "I don't understand any of this. The book has been leading us so far, and suddenly, it goes silent. It doesn't make any sense."

"You know," he said, turning to look at her. "I could do with some real food for a change; I'm sick of eating all these fruits."

"I don't know what we can do except to try to find a way out ourselves. Perhaps, the book wants us to trust our own judgment now."

He looked at her seriously for a while and said, "Rachel, what is the matter? Something's bothering you. You look like you didn't sleep at all last night."

"I can't put my finger on it, but I believe I'm not yet getting the point of this whole thing."

"What do you mean?"

"I hardly know, myself. But I know there's more to this…" she said, pointing towards the book, "than meets the eye."

"Well, I'm sure I don't know what it is, but we won't know unless we get a move on. I think we should head north."

"I don't see why we shouldn't," Rachel said, plaiting her hair into a ponytail. She wondered how she looked.

Brian sported a few days' growth under his chin. His hair was unkempt, and his clothes looked ragged, but to Rachel, he still looked as handsome as ever. She wondered how she looked as she hadn't seen a mirror since they crashed.

"Any ideas what one could eat besides apples and pears?" she asked, though not really expecting him to come up with anything. The land seemed bare of meat despite its beauty.

"Well, if I had a rifle, we might look for some deer. I did it in camp. But as it is…" His voice trailed off, and his eyes suddenly widened. "Of course!"

"What is it?"

"I don't know why we didn't think of it before. The river! I've got my knife. We could find some trout."

Rachel smiled enthusiastically. "That would surely make a great change from apples. But we don't have a fishing line."

"That should be no problem," he smiled confidently and reached for his backpack to retrieve his pocket knife. He snapped his fingers. "All I have to do is sing to the fish, and they will follow me."

She got up and followed him as they walked down to the river. "Just like that, huh?" she teased. "I salute you, oh… You,

108

charmer of fishes."

"Thank you, my lady," he said with a mock bow, and they both laughed.

Catching the fish was not as easy as Brian had predicted. However, the fish were close to the edge of the river, and he was able to bend down to spear a few of them with his knife. They just seemed to swarm around him.

Rachel watched him in fascination and admiration as he speared half a dozen trout and cleaned them thoroughly. Then he built a fire and began to roast the trout.

"Do they teach you all this in camp?" she asked.

"Yes," he replied, turning the fish over with his knife. "And a whole lot more."

"Maybe I'll go next year..." Rachel said but didn't add '*if we ever get out of here.*'

"Sure. But the camp I went to was for boys only. But I hear there's this neat girl's camp in Wyoming."

"Yeah, and all they'll do there is try not to get their nails dirty," Rachel scoffed.

Brian smiled. "I think they do a whole lot more than that. They are pretty good at tracking, and they hunt. They spend a lot of time on the shooting range too. They're all crack shots."

"Ugh, who would want to do that?" Rachel said with a shudder. She had a phobia for guns and shooting of any kind, whether for sport or pleasure.

"Well, I don't know, but I suppose any girl who wouldn't mind getting her nails dirty," Brian mused with a sly grin. He turned the fish over. "My, do these look delicious!" he beamed.

And so it was. The best food they'd had in six days, which they both thoroughly enjoyed. They almost felt normal again.

*****

Francis heard the voice from like a thousand miles away.

"Francis! Francis, wake up, or you'll be late," the voice was saying.

His eyelids felt very heavy. He wanted to wake up, but it seemed like a great effort just to open his eyes.

"Francis!" his mother yelled again. This time, he forced himself to open his eyes. The sunlight was already streaming in through the windows. He glanced at his sheets, which were hopelessly tangled. He had not had a restful night.

"Francis!" his mother yelled.

"I'm coming already," he mumbled as he got out of bed and hurried to the bathroom. He deliberately avoided looking at the clock. No sense getting himself more panicked than necessary.

About fifteen minutes later, he was out of the house and on his way to school. As he sat on the bus, he thought over the events of the night before. He had had the same dream three times running. It always started the same way.

Tess, he, and his mother were at home watching TV, and suddenly, there was the acrid smell of smoke in the house. His mother tried to go into the kitchen to investigate, but the smoke was too much. Covering her nose and mouth, she motioned for him to get out of the house.

They both ran out of the house together, but it seemed like Tess ran into her room to get something. They were both screaming for her to come out when the house was set ablaze, and Tess was trapped. The house became a raging inferno, and Francis and his mother watched in horror as the firefighters tried in vain to put out the fire.

No matter what they did, it just kept getting worse. And they screamed themselves hoarse, crying out Tess' name, but there was no answer. The nightmare continued until he woke up.

He wanted to dismiss it, but it seemed too vivid to ignore. He wished he could understand what it meant, however, the meaning seemed to elude him. He just knew that he had to get in touch with his sister, somehow, and find out if she was alright. But, without having a clue where she could be, how was he going to do that?

*****

Donna woke up feeling refreshed. She'd not felt like this in days, not since she heard the news about Brian missing. She looked over at the other side of the bed. It was empty, which meant Kevin was already up. Or had he ever gone to sleep? She wasn't sure.

She slipped on her robe and walked into the kitchen to find him brewing a pot of coffee. His eyes were red-rimmed and sunken, like he had not slept in days, which was actually the case.

"Good morning, Kevin," she said pleasantly.

"Well, someone is definitely looking bright and perky this morning. You sleep well, honey?" he asked with a mug in his hand, trying to smile.

"Great. And you?"

"Like a baby," he said sarcastically, turning his face from her. *A colicky baby*, she thought.

She went to him and tried to ease the tension in his shoulders by massaging them. "We'll find them soon, honey. We will," she said softly.

"Did God tell you that?" Kevin mocked and then regretted his sharpness almost immediately.

Donna sighed. "Not really, but when I prayed, I felt a sort of peace, like an assurance that they were safe. It's been a long time since I prayed. I haven't prayed since my mother died, and I didn't know what to say, but I felt Someone was listening to me. I don't know how I know, but I'm convinced that they're fine."

"Yeah, yeah... How do you want your coffee, honey? Black or with sugar?" he asked, pouring out a cup. She varied her choices depending on her mood and the diet she was on.

She felt hurt by his abrupt dismissal. "Black," she muttered in a barely audible voice.

He held out a cup to her and looked deep into her eyes. "Let's hope you're right, Donna. Let's hope to God you're right," he added softly.

*****

Mary poured herself another cup of coffee and plopped on the kitchen stool. She knew she needed to begin searching for Tess, but she had no idea where to start. She'd already called up a few of Tess's friends that she knew, but they were as blank as she was on Tess's whereabouts.

She was a bit wary of involving the police, especially if Tess had broken the law. Maybe she had stolen a car or robbed a bank or something. You never knew with Tess. But then, she considered which was better: being uncertain whether her daughter might spend some time behind bars or being uncertain whether she'll ever see her again?

Mary took a deep breath and made a quick decision. She picked up the phone, dialed a number, and said, "Good morning, I'd like to talk to the officer in charge, please. Yes, I'd like to file a missing person's report."

She listened for a few minutes and then said, "Okay, I'll hold."

As she waited, she hoped with all her heart that she wasn't making a big mistake. She wished she could be sure that, with this call, she wasn't sending Tess to jail.

16

Chapter 16

Rachel had to admit to herself that she had overeaten. She felt too heavy to move and kept telling Brian to slow down, even though they had only walked about three miles. They kept heading north as they got no direction from the book.

"Brian, wait!" she called out again, as she collapsed onto the ground. She felt like she could use a nap.

Brian walked back to where she was and sat down beside her. "At this rate, we'll be going nowhere fast," he smiled.

"Just give me five minutes," she said apologetically.

He leaned towards her. "You know, I really don't think it would be a good idea for you to go to any camp at all. You would find it very difficult to cope," he said facetiously.

She glared at him. "You were the one who stuffed me with trout."

"You were the one who kept saying you were hungry," he retorted.

"Alright, that does it," she said resolutely and got up. "March!" She began to move forward.

"Rachel, what are you doing?"

"I'm trying to show you that I can hold my own. I'm no wimp," she said fiercely.

"Oh, sit down, Rachel," Brian said, smiling at her, contrite. "I didn't mean to suggest that you were anything like that."

"No, no, let's go on Brian," she said, shaking her head, her jaw set. "We've got a long way to go as it is..."

He pulled her towards him, his face filled with amusement. "I love you, Rachel Menendez, even when you act as stubborn as a pack mule."

Rachel was not amused. "Brian Anderson, let go of me this instant!" She struggled to free herself from his embrace.

"Come on, Rachel. Try to be reasonable..." he said while trying to strengthen his grip on her arm.

Without any warning, the ground underneath them split open, and they fell straight down into a large hole.

*****

Sierra had wanted to go to work that morning, but she'd changed her mind. She'd called in sick again and hoped that she would not be fired from her jobs. Her managers were understanding and had told her to take as much time as she needed. She had promised herself she would try to act as normal as possible, but it seemed that she just couldn't. Not when she felt like her heart had been ripped out,

She absently sipped a cup of coffee and contemplated what she would do with her day. It was nearly afternoon, and she had taken to sitting by the phone with the TV blaring, staring at nothing. But she didn't want to keep doing that. There was nothing to be gained by that.

She wished her mom were around so she could ask her what

to do. Mom had always been so wise, so loving, so forgiving. But that was before she had succumbed to cancer. Colon cancer, a terrible disease. She had watched her mother die a slow and painful death, but she was glad they were on speaking terms before she died. She had sat in the hospital, helplessly watching her mother die. Was she going to do the same with her daughter?

Sierra had thought to travel to Brazil herself and search for Rachel, but the resources she had at hand were limited. She wished she could do something productive in the search for her daughter, but everyone had told her that the best she could do was to sit by the phone and pray, and let the police do their work. Well, she was sick of sitting down by the phone and doing nothing.

She threw the remnants of the coffee into the sink. Her mind was made up. She would do something. With her jaw set, and her chin firm, she went to the shower.

She would go to the Andersons' house and speak to Brian's mother. It was their children that were missing after all. Together, they could come up with a plan.

*****

"Mom, we've got to find Tess," Francis said abruptly as soon as he got home from school and plopped down on the sofa beside his mother.

Mary blinked at him. "Yeah, I've been feeling the same. I even called the police today."

"And what did they say?"

"That they'll start looking. But why have you gotten so worried all of a sudden?"

Francis sighed. "I've been having these horrible dreams. And they're all about Tess being in some danger. I'm scared for her,

116

Mom."

His mother pulled him close. "Remember what you told me the other day. It's going to be alright, Francis. You'll see."

Francis desperately wanted to believe it, and so did Mary.

The shrill sound of the phone's ring pierced through them, and Mary snapped her head to it. Her heart raced in anticipation as she lunged to pick it. Francis held his breath, his eyes locked with his mothers.'

"We know where your daughter went," a voice on the other end said.

*****

Rachel seemed shell-shocked. Brian was the first to find his voice.

"What in God's name just happened?" he asked no one in particular.

They were in a deep, dark hole. However, he couldn't estimate how deep it was. *At least eight feet*, he thought. How were they supposed to get out of there?

"There's got to be a way out," Rachel said desperately, as if reading his thoughts. She began to feel her way around the pit, hoping to find a crevice, an opening of some sort. But she couldn't find anything that encouraged her in her supposition that they would get out.

"This is impossible," Brian said after he had also felt his way around.

They had no source of light; his flashlight had given out eons ago. There were no handholds or footholds that he could see that would help them climb out of the pit. No way of calling out for help. They were stuck for good, this time. It was like they had been buried alive.

*****

Donna didn't know exactly how to receive Rachel's mother. Should she call Kevin? He had just gone to check on a few things at work. But even if she called him, what would he do? She stared at the woman for a few seconds after she opened the door. Then she realized she was being rude.

"I'm sorry, Mrs. Menendez. Do come in," she said, trying to be gracious. "I wasn't expecting company."

Sierra was abashed. She recalled exactly how she behaved the last time she was there. She'd acted just like a female lioness that had been robbed of one of her cubs. She hoped Donna understood that.

"Your house is really beautiful," she said while glancing appreciatively at her surroundings as she took a seat. She had had little time or patience to admit it the other day.

"Thank you," Donna muttered. "But I am sure you did not come here just to admire my decor."

Sierra sighed. Maybe they should start over.

"Look, Mrs. Anderson. I'm aware that I acted rather strangely when I came to your house the other night-"

"Strangely?" Donna asked, smiling like that wasn't quite the case.

"Alright, maybe even unkindly," Sierra admitted.

"Unkindly?" Donna asked with a twinkle in her eyes.

Sierra groaned inwardly. "Alright, I was really rude. Satisfied?" she said, a little sharply.

To her surprise, Donna, who was sitting directly in front of her, reached over and patted her knee.

"You did nothing out of the ordinary, Mrs. Menendez. You did exactly what I would have done if I were you. In fact, I might have acted worse. It's perfectly understandable."

For the first time since she entered the Andersons' home, Sierra smiled. She had not made a mistake by coming here. They were both on the same page.

"Now, to my first question... Mrs. Menendez, how can I help you this fine day?"

Sierra smiled. "For starters, you can call me Sierra."

"Alright, Sierra. Please feel free to call me Donna."

"Thanks, Donna, I'll get right to it."

*****

"Brian, we've got to do something!" Rachel said frantically. She was finding it difficult to think clearly. This was so unlike anything she had ever experienced before. There was nowhere to run or hide. They were trapped.

Brian didn't answer. He had no clue what they could do. She removed the book from her backpack but found she couldn't see a word. Their salvation was not in the book this time.

Unbidden, tears ran down her cheeks. They were at their wits' end. They were going to die like rats in the hole. There was no way out now. She choked back a sob.

Brian heard her and put an arm awkwardly around her shoulder. "Shh. Don't cry, Rachel. It's going to be okay." But she stiffened under his touch. He did not even believe what he was saying. Empty words that meant nothing.

"Rachel, I know you don't feel like it now, but we've got to make ourselves comfortable. Let's sit or lie down. Maybe something will happen, or we'll figure out a way to escape this hellhole..." His voice was pleading and desperate, as if willing her to believe him.

Rachel said nothing but, feeling her way around, sat down. Brian held her hand and sat down too. And for the life of them, neither of them could think of what to say. They were both silent, trapped, and helpless.

17

Chapter 17

"Well, I don't know about you, Sierra," Donna began after they had both taken two glasses of orange juice. "But I have found that praying has helped me during this period."

Sierra almost choked on her orange juice. "Praying?" she sputtered. "I wouldn't have taken you as the praying kind."

Donna smiled sadly. "Neither would I. I was a Christian once, though. I believed in God and the death of Christ on the cross. That was when I was in high school. That was before my mother got sick and died."

"So, what happened after that?" Sierra asked.

"I asked God to heal my mother. I prayed and prayed for days and told God how much I needed her. I wept endlessly. But in the end, it seemed that her illness was stronger than me and all my prayers."

"What did you do then?" Sierra asked, leaning forward.

"I told God that since He had refused to intervene on my mother's behalf, I would no longer need Him. My mother was a strong Christian and had taught me we can't always understand

God or His ways. But I didn't see how God's plans made any sense.

"My mother was everything to me, and...well, my father was my father. He remarried, and for a long time, I resented both him and his new wife. I was terribly unhappy until I met Kevin. He was like my savior. And all these years, I thought he was all I needed."

"Well, I think I've always been a Christian," Sierra said haltingly. "I've always gone to church, since I was a kid. I'm not much for praying, but I go to confession regularly. I'm no saint, but I dare say I'm better than some people..."

"Perhaps," Donna muttered slowly, "my definition and your definition of Christianity are rather different. But, then again, I haven't told you how I developed a renewed interest in praying."

"I'm all ears."

"When Brian disappeared, I was more frightened than I had ever been in my life. I turned to my husband. My husband did everything in his power. He called all the important people he knew. Interpol was called. We worried, but no one could find them. For the first time, I realized my husband was inadequate. He could fail me, just like any other human being."

"And then you turned to God? I thought He had already failed you."

"That's what I thought too. But as it turns out, I was wrong. A few months after my mother died, a woman, who I never knew, sent me a letter and told me my mother had changed her life. It turned out they were both in the same hospital ward. My mother's bravery and witness for Christ struck her, and she gave her life to the Lord, and this gave her the courage to face death and whatever came after.

"At first, I discounted the letter and other letters like it. I was in no mood to hear any such thing. But lately, I've been reminded of the verse, "*Unless a grain of wheat falls into the ground and dies, it cannot bear much fruit...*"

"So, you're saying...?" Sierra asked, lost.

"I'm saying, my mom was that grain of wheat. It seemed like more people were inspired by how she faced death than throughout her lifetime."

"Oh," Sierra muttered, doubtful.

"But what made me sure that her death was the right thing was that this morning, I heard the laughter," Donna said, smiling in recollection.

"The laughter?" Sierra was clueless.

Donna giggled. "My mom had a way of laughing when she was extremely happy. Her laugh was deep-throated, full, and extremely infectious, and I heard it this morning. It seemed to tell me that she was happy, and I rejoiced because looking back now, I realize that in the latter periods of her life, even before she got ill, she had little opportunity for that laughter."

"Hmmm..." Sierra was unsure how to respond.

"But, Sierra," Donna said earnestly. "I'm beginning to think the issue is not whether I can rationalize or explain everything that God allows. The real issue is whether I'm willing to trust Him even when I can't understand. He is, after all, my Creator."

Sierra looked bewildered. All this religious talk was making her feel very uncomfortable.

"All this must be very confusing for you," Donna said gently, as if reading Sierra's thoughts. "I don't understand it fully myself, but I learn something new every day when I read my Bible." Donna's face took on a wistful expression. Then she turned back to her friend and said abruptly, "Sierra, I'm sorry we got side-tracked by my story. Let's get back to the issue at hand. What do you suppose we do about our children?"

Sierra could only sigh in response.

*****

Mary wondered what on earth she was going to do about her daughter when she got off the phone.

"Your sister went to Brazil," she told Francis in a matter-of-fact tone.

"What?"

"Apparently, she and a few other kids decided to go to Brazil for a summer getaway."

"It sounds just like her," Francis said, scrunching his eyebrows. "So, when is she going to come back?"

"You see, there's just a little problem. They're looking for them right now."

"What is that supposed to mean?"

"They traveled in a private plane. They should have been in Brazil by now, but it turns out they're not. The other parents are looking for their kids too."

"That means they could be anywhere by now. Looks like we're back to square one, Mom. We don't really know where she is."

"Well, if I know Tess, she's probably found a way to get them all into trouble. They'll call soon from wherever they are."

"Mom, I hope you're right. But what if Tess has run away for good this time?" Francis asked, looking scared.

"Don't worry, Francis," Mary said, with a confidence she did not feel. "Everything will be fine. We'll find her."

*****

She was at the river. The cool, clear river, shimmering in the sun. Rachel stood beside it, watching her reflection. She looked very beautiful in her white dress and hat. A Celina Dior collection, quite fetching indeed.

But suddenly, the reflections gave way to past events in her life, and she was watching it just like a movie; every unkind word and deed she had ever done. Every picture, every scene seemed to muddy the clear water. She was seeing it again, she realized. She was filled with remorse all over again. Waves of shame swept over her. Just when she could bear it no longer and was turning away, she felt a hand clamp on her shoulder.

"Where do you think you're going, Miss?" a man's deep voice said roughly.

She spun around to face him but could not see his face. He wore a black hat and a long black coat, and he was much taller than her.

"I was just..." she began.

"Just what?" he thundered, shaking her. "Don't you see that you have poisoned our clean and clear water? You have ruined it!"

Rachel gulped in fright. "I'm sorry, Sir. I didn't mean to," she said in a small voice.

"Being sorry does not help anything," he shouted, still holding her by the shoulders. "You have polluted this water, and now, you shall have to cleanse it."

Rachel did not know how she could possibly do that. This man frightened her, and he was putting so much weight on her shoulders, she was beginning to feel a strain in them. He was hurting her!

"I'm sorry, Sir," she said again, "but I have no idea-"

"You mean, you don't know how? I'll show you how!" he boomed, and so saying, he dragged her by her hair up the river's edge. She stifled a cry of pain and glanced at the river in horror.

It had turned from a muddy brown to a dark red. It looked just like...blood. The man pushed her down until her head was bent over the river.

"You will have to suck the poison out of the river," he said, menacingly.

Rachel's mind didn't want to register his words, but his intent was clear as he bent her head over the water. *He wants me to drink this?* But it was impossible. She knew with absolute certainty that if she drank it, she would die.

"Please," she said, with as much courage as she could muster. But the man pretended not to hear. He only bent her lower and lower until her face was very close to the bloodied water. So close that some of it splashed her white dress. A sickening smell filled her nostrils. The smell of rotting flesh.

"Drink!" he ordered.

"N-O-O-O!" she screamed at the top of her lungs.

And then Brian was by her side, holding her arm. "What is it?" he asked.

Suddenly, she was no longer by the river but in a dark pit.

"My God, Rachel, what happened? You screamed so loudly," he remonstrated.

Rachel was still too shaken by her dream to answer. It had been a horrible nightmare. But she had woken up from that nightmare only to awaken to this one; this living nightmare.

"Rachel, talk to me. You're scaring me," Brian pleaded.

But she couldn't. She began to cry, great choking sobs that racked her entire body. The man had been right. She had polluted the river. She was dirty. She was filthy. She was unworthy.

Brian wished she wouldn't cry so. But the flood of tears didn't seem like they'd stop soon.

Then from somewhere deep within her, she cried out, "God, I'm sorry! I'm so sorry!" she wept. "Please help me. Don't let him kill me!"

Brian didn't know what to make of it. "Rachel, what happened? What did you do?"

"Oh, God... Brian," she said, holding his shoulder. "It was horrible. All those things I did at the river. The man wanted to kill me, and he was right. I was dirty. I am so dirty."

Brian was more confused than ever.

"All the evil things I've done, Brian, I wish I'd never done them. But I did, and I must be punished for them. I think that's why the man threw us into the pit and left us here to die."

If Brian had been frightened before, he was made even more frightened by Rachel's incoherent babblings.

"God, I'm sorry! Please, don't let me die; don't let us die. I know I don't deserve it, but please, have mercy! Forgive me," she cried repeatedly.

Brian tried to soothe her, but it seemed she wouldn't be calmed. Brian began to think they might never make it out of the hole alive.

Exhausted with all her crying, Rachel drifted into sleep. And after a few minutes, Brian, lulled by her gentle and even breathing, drifted off to sleep himself.

18

Chapter 18

onna dropped the receiver and sat down on the sofa to think. Kevin had taken to his study and did not feel like talking. After talking with Sierra, she had decided to contact the other parents.

Mary, Tess's mother, seemed to have taken the news of her daughter's disappearance calmly enough; too calmly, Donna thought. She had told Donna, without the slightest hesitation, that Tess was known to disappear for days on end and, without a doubt, would return home soon.

"She does what she wants," Mary said. "And then returns home afterwards. I can't seem to manage the girl, and she doesn't listen to anyone."

Donna thought that was too bad and wished she could take as nonchalant a view as Mary. Craig's mother, on the other hand, was very distressed. Patricia thought her dear boy had abandoned her, and as she spoke, it was evident that he was his mama's darling. The two mothers, however, did not seem to think, as she had, that any great misfortune had befallen their children and felt confident that they would find their way back home.

The way they spoke made her wonder. Had they really run away? Was Brian at this very moment having some joyride with his friends and not giving a thought to what his parents might be thinking or feeling?

But she refused to entertain such thoughts. He had everything he needed at home; they had not denied him freedom. He had plans for himself; plans that included Yale and a bright future. He had more to lose by running away.

She was glad of Sierra's visit. At least they had become friends, and she would look for other opportunities to strengthen their friendship, but she wished Sierra had had good news to report.

The facts were their children had been missing for nearly a week, and no one, even after using the most sophisticated search systems available, had an idea where they were. But she decided to consider more than just the bare facts. Somewhere within her heart, a voice was whispering, "*Can you not trust Me with them?*" She knew she had no other option.

*****

Sally held her weeping mother in her arms.

"How could Craig do this to us?" her mother sobbed. "It's not fair."

"Mom, you can't talk like that. Craig didn't abandon us. He wouldn't do that," Sally said, trying to stop the tears that wanted to spill off her cheeks.

"He said he wasn't interested in the family business. He must have felt choked here."

"Mom," Sally remonstrated. "You mustn't blame yourself. Besides, Craig never did much work around here anyway. He could never complain that you were working him too hard. Let's just have a little faith that he'll be coming back to us."

"Oh, Craig!" Patricia wept as Sally watched her and bit her lip.

Sally didn't know what to think. Could Craig really have run away? Or had something more sinister happened? She just wished she could talk to her little brother and find out if he was alright.

*****

Rachel stirred in her sleep. Her eyelids seemed rather heavy, and when she opened her eyes, she couldn't help feeling the sun was too bright.

The sun is too bright!

The thought made her sit up suddenly. She could see the sun. She was still in the dark pit, which had ceased to be dark any longer, but she could see it.

She shook Brian, who still slept a few feet away from her, and whose form she could see perfectly. "Brian, get up!" she said, shouting into his ear.

Brian gave a great big yawn and tried to continue his sleep, but she shook him so persistently, he was forced to open his eyes. And he too sat bolt upright.

"Oh my God!" he exclaimed. Not only could they see the sun and an opening in that formerly dark pit, but there were also some footholds on the walls of the pit, which Brian would have sworn were not there before. But then again, they had not had the advantage of light to be absolutely sure.

"Does this mean what I think it means?" he asked Rachel excitedly.

"It means God heard my prayer after all, and we won't have to die in this pit! Oh, God, thank You!" Rachel said.

"It means we can get out of here!" Brian responded.

By a series of maneuverings, they managed to get hold of the first foothold. It was difficult, and even though Brian tried to support her from below, she nearly fell a couple of times. But they got to the last foothold, and Rachel was able to clamber out of the pit, with Brian following behind her.

Once out of the pit, they hugged each other in relief, and Brian let out a whoop. It was indeed a bright and glorious morning after that night in the pit.

"Man, am I glad to be out of that hell-hole!" he said.

Rachel had the same sentiments but added, "God certainly came to our rescue."

Brian nodded but didn't say more. He was beginning to think they had nine lives. They needed to figure out the next step. But he wondered how many more surprises lurked on their journey.

"Let's get something to eat first, and then we can decide where to go," Rachel suggested.

"Trout?" he asked with a wink.

"No, thank you. I think I've had my share for a while."

They walked about the park and found some apples, and after eating almost half a dozen each, they sat down to deliberate on their next move.

"Should we see what the book has to say?" Rachel proposed.

"Nah, I think we should just continue north. We should be able to find some people around. Besides, the book has been silent all this while. I think it is no longer useful to us."

"You never know," Rachel said and went on to open the book anyway. She flipped through its pages, not expecting to find anything, but was surprised to read:

"*Go east of the sixth apple tree from the river, wherein you will find a glen, and therein, your liberation.*"

"What does it say?" Brian asked, noting the intense look on her face. She read it aloud to him.

"What does liberation mean? Does it mean we are finally going to be out of here?" he wondered aloud.

"I want to believe so," Rachel said.

"It has to be!" Brian remarked. "The only way we can be liberated is if we can get back home. Finally!"

With a flourish, he got up and held out his hand to Rachel. "Shall we?" he asked.

She stood up and took his proffered hand, and they walked towards the river, trying to locate the sixth apple tree.

*****

Sierra wanted to put the conversation she had with Donna out of her mind. All that talk about God and trust. She had never been that close to God before, even though she had gone to a good Catholic school. And trust? She had lost that since Luis left her. She had found out quite early in life that it was better not to believe in anything than to believe in something that was not going to happen. It hurt less that way.

As regards Donna, well, folks always had to find ways of comforting themselves, she thought. Sighing, she switched on the TV and spent twenty minutes staring at nothing.

She glanced at her white Bible, lying on the mantle-piece, covered with dust. It hadn't been opened in years, not even when she went to church once every month for confession. On impulse, she took it from its place and wiped off the dust on it with her hand. She opened its cover gingerly.

Now, what was that strange verse Donna talked about? She asked herself. *Something about a grain of wheat dying...*

*****

They walked through the trees carefree and laughing. Brian knew deep within that they were getting out of this nightmare, and Rachel felt the same. They'd gone all the way down; only good things could happen from here.

"The book sounded really weird using words like glen and therein. Do you know what a glen looks like?" Rachel asked.

"It's a kind of enclosed place or something. I don't know, but I guess we'll know it when we see it. Don't worry about it, chipmunk," he said, tweaking her ear.

"I am not a chipmunk," she rejected in mock indignation.

"I never meant you were, darling..." Brian circled a tree and presented Rachel with some flowers he had gotten for her, when she wasn't looking, and bowed.

"Well, aren't you becoming Prince Charming..." Rachel said, smiling.

Brian stared at her in mock surprise. "I thought that's what I'd always been."

"No," Rachel replied curtly, raising her eyebrows. "You've been more like a pain in the neck, but that pain is actually getting to feel kind of pleasant."

He leaned close to her. "Really? Well, you, my dear, are actually causing me to feel severe pain here," he said, pointing to his chest, down towards his heart. "It aches like crazy, but then, I've never been happier."

You're beginning to transfer that particular sort of pain to me, Rachel thought. *And I don't mind at all; not one bit.*

"Race you to the glen," Brian said suddenly and began to run.

"Oh, come on, you don't even know how far it is," Rachel protested.

"That's why we've got to get there faster. Come on," Brian

urged.

Reluctantly, Rachel began to jog.

*****

Kevin stared at his wife in disbelief as she set the table. Had the waiting driven her mad?

"How you can act so calm when we haven't seen them in nearly a week is beyond me," he said as she placed a cup of coffee before him.

Donna sat down and sipped her coffee, then said, "Well, unlike you, Kev, I have the advantage of knowing." She knew he wouldn't understand, but it did not lessen the conviction she felt.

"Knowing what?"

"That they're going to be alright."

"You say it like you're so certain."

She placed her hand on his and looked straight into his eyes. "There's a thinking, Kevin, and there's a knowing. I know."

Kevin knew the time had come to share what had been burning inside him. He needed to get it out. "I'm so sorry, Donna. This is all my fault. You warned me," he said softly, his eyes downcast.

Donna stared at him; her eyes filled with tears as she threw her arms around him. "Shh. Don't blame yourself, dear. None of us could have predicted this would happen. Besides, they are going to be just fine."

Kevin hugged his wife tightly, desperately wanting to believe she was right.

19

Chapter 19

Francis and Tess sat beside the river with their feet dangling in the water. Tess told him a joke she had heard at school, and he laughed so hard, his sides ached. It felt so good to spend time with her. It had been too long since they had spent time together. Then she suddenly announced that she was going for a swim.

"Do you think you should?" Francis asked cautiously. "We don't really know how deep this thing is."

"Oh, you worry too much, little brother," she said with a carefree smile and jumped in.

She began to swim with broad powerful strokes and then called out, "The water's really cool, Francis. Why don't you jump in?"

"Nah," Francis said. He didn't really feel like swimming.

"Oh, come on…" she was saying when she suddenly began to go underwater. It was as if she was being sucked under.

"Tess! Tess!" he cried in horror, but the only response he could get was her flailing arms struggling to stay afloat. He couldn't see her, but he heard a voice say, "She's gone, Francis.

But it's not too late for you. Not yet."

Then he woke up. He sat in bed, panting. Francis had no idea what the dream could mean. But all he could determine was that it made him feel cold all over.

*****

There it is, Rachel thought as they reached what looked like a grove. It was enclosed, secluded, and there seemed to be a haunting beauty about it. There was a small opening that looked as if it had been cut out. This was their way to freedom.

"You're ready?" Brian asked, excitedly.

"Uh-huh," she said, even though she didn't know if she was. Taking her hand, they stepped through the opening together.

A whole new world awaited them. A new world of green. The grass had never appeared greener to them, and in the center were two wooden poles splinted together and surrounded by flowers.

They stared at the scene without saying anything. They looked around, but there was nothing else to be seen. No means of exit, just those wooden poles stuck together in the shape of a cross, for no reason...

Rachel and Brian both glanced at each other in sudden comprehension. It was a cross... It symbolized the crucifixion and resurrection of Christ! Brian could not help swearing under his breath, and he threw his hands up in the air.

"I can't believe this," he grunted, raking a hand through his hair. "This must be some kind of joke. It's a game. We were set up by some religious nut! Everything we went through was just so we could come here? That's crazy!"

Rachel was too bewildered to know what to think or say. Nothing in her entire life had prepared her for what she faced in the last few days. And these wooden poles were supposed to be their liberation...? But how was that possible?

"Come on, Rachel, let's get out of here," Brian said resolutely. "There's got to be a way out of this place, and we're not playing these games anymore. Let's find our own way out of this nightmare."

"Brian, wait," she said, glancing at the wood. It looked so fine and smooth, and she wondered what kind of artistic, religious nut would have put it there. She ran her hands over the wood. It was hard and smooth and strong. She looked for rough edges, but there was none. Then she paused, awestruck.

"Rachel, are you coming or not?" Brian asked impatiently, already beginning to walk away. Rachel couldn't answer. She was too busy watching the scene before her.

A man was kneeling there by the cross, weeping. He was sweating profusely too, and the sweat was of a strange red color. She felt rather than heard his words: "Oh, if it be Your will, let this cup pass over me..." His voice was low and agonized.

Rachel trembled when she heard a powerful voice ask, "What about Rachel?"

The man lifted his eyes to heaven and murmured, "For Rachel, I will do anything. I love her. Not my will, but Yours."

Then he got up and kept muttering to himself, "For Rachel, for Rachel..." as he walked away.

"Rache, we've got to get going," Brian said, beginning to get angry.

Rachel answered, as if in a dream, "Go on ahead, Brian. I'll meet you."

Brian snorted and walked off while Rachel sat by the cross, wondering. Why did that man say he loved her? Why would he love her? What had she done that he seemed ready to do anything for her? He sounded like he was going to die or something awful was going to happen to him. Was he going to die for her?

"I already have," a voice said behind her. She knew it was the man, but when she looked over her shoulder, there was no one there. And immediately He said it, her heart felt strangely full. She felt that she loved Him too; this Man who was willing to die for her – who had died for her.

"I love you too," she said softly and ran her hands over the wooden poles again, this time lovingly, with tears streaking her cheeks. Was it true what she had always been told; that Jesus had died for her sins? He must have been the man she had seen.

She had found it incomprehensible all her life, but now, in the light of all she had seen, it made perfect sense. Suddenly, the grass she was standing on seemed unsteady. Her hands started to shake, and she tried to hold on to the wood. But before she knew it, she was falling, falling...

*****

Brian picked up some wild berries and placed them in his mouth. Although they were fresh and juicy, he frowned. Where was Rachel? She should have been with him by now. He was very upset at their wasted journey. Sad to discover it had been a game after all. Someone out there was trying to manipulate them, and as for him, he refused to be made a fool of any longer.

He began to feel uneasy. Perhaps she had wandered off somewhere without taking note of the direction he had taken. He felt a little guilty that he had left her alone.

He decided to go back for her, calling her name as he walked back to the glen. He finally got to the glen and stepped inside, but she was not there. What was more, her backpack was lying on the ground. Where would she have gone without her backpack?

It didn't seem like a good sign. But she couldn't have gone far without it. Tired and frustrated, he sat down to wait. She would have to come back. She wouldn't go anywhere without the book.

*****

Sierra felt more confused than ever. She had taken the Bible to her priest during her monthly confession, hoping he would be able to explain Donna's strange words, but he only muttered something about it being figurative and seemed as clueless as she was.

What exactly did a "*seed falling into the ground and dying*" mean? Was it God's way of telling her that her daughter was going to die? Was her daughter falling into the ground and dying at this very moment? She wished she could know for sure.

Donna would know, but she felt hesitant to approach her on the subject. She didn't want Donna to think she was taking this God thing seriously. But was she? She wasn't quite sure what to think.

*****

Sally and her mother sat by the phone, hoping for news. But there was none. Or at least, no positive news. The police had already been instructed to start looking for bodies, and the situation seemed grim.

There was a report of a plane crash over the area Craig and his friends were supposed to have traveled, but their bodies had not been discovered. Sally and her mother were trying to get themselves prepared for the worst. But Patricia was taking things very hard, and Sally felt she was about to come apart at the seams.

"Mom," Sally found herself saying after hours of waiting that day. "As hard as this is for you, it's hard for me too. But I need you to be strong, Mom. Whatever happens, we must be grateful we have each other. Craig would want us to remember that."

Sally felt helpless as her mother burst into a fresh round of tears on hearing Craig's name. When would all the pain and uncertainty end?

20

Chapter 20

Rachel felt gentle hands placing her down on the ground. Unlike her last free fall through the earth, this ride felt as though she was guided. She looked around her and admired the lush greenery. She knew she was in a forest, but it was unlike anyone she had ever seen. It was not at all like where she and Brian had been.

Flowers grew in profusion here, the fruit trees seemed to cover almost every square inch, and different furry animals scurried around. If she could ever have imagined the Garden of Eden, she couldn't have imagined anything better. But as beautiful as her surroundings were, she couldn't help feeling a slight panic.

Where was she? And how would Brian find her? And her backpack, the book... She got up from the ground, suddenly frightened.

"Shh. All that doesn't matter now," the voice said.

She knew it was the Man, but He had this uncanny way of speaking without warning. And she couldn't see Him. But what did He mean by it didn't matter? How could Brian not matter? Would she ever see him again?

"I gave My all for you. Aren't you willing to give him up for Me?" the Man asked.

Rachel wondered how He knew her thoughts, but, of course, as she was starting to learn, He was God. She didn't understand what He meant by giving up Brian. Why would she have to do that?

"Whoever wants to be My disciple must deny himself, take up his cross, and follow Me," He said.

Rachel was confused. She did not like this at all. "Where are You?" she asked aloud.

"Right beside you, always," He replied, and this time, it was like He was speaking into her ear. "Rachel, this part of the journey, you will have to undertake on your own. Come, you have much to learn..." Then she felt gentle hands pulling her forward.

"But, what about the book?" she asked lamely. How could she continue her journey without the book? She felt it was her ticket to the real world.

"You do not need it any longer because now you have Me. I am the Book," the voice said.

*****

"Sierra, I have to confess to you that I don't know exactly what it means either," Donna sighed, glancing at her friend, who looked more than a little perplexed. Sierra had gone to visit Donna again, in search of some answers.

"Don't know what it means?" Sierra repeated.

"Yes. That's because it could have many meanings, and in our situation, I'm unsure what it represents... A seed falling into the ground and dying might mean literal death, like Jesus' death did, or it might mean dying to self, or it might just mean a trial we have to pass through in order to produce fruit, like saying, 'no pain, no gain...'"

Sierra stared at her for a moment, then said, "I'm lost. What do you mean by dying to self?"

"Sometimes, God requires that we give up everything to follow Him, but in giving up all, we receive a lot more. For us to receive life, we must die to those things that enslave us. Think of it this way; let's say you're a chain smoker. Then, one day, you go to the doctor's for an annual checkup, and the doctor tells you that you are at risk of developing lung cancer. He advises you to quit smoking. Won't you try to stop smoking to save your life? Going cold turkey might be so difficult at first, you might be 'dying' for a smoke, but you find out that in giving up smoking, you have gained a lot more; your life."

Sierra nodded imperceptibly. "I think I understand a little. But I don't see what this has to do with my daughter."

"I'm not sure either, but I think we will soon find out," Donna said gravely. She really hoped it would be soon.

*****

"Mom, there's something I think you should know," Francis said. He was standing in the doorway of his mother's bedroom, watching her fold clothes into the wardrobe.

"What is it, Francis?"

"I think you should sit down for this, Mom, just in case."

Mary took a good look at her son and then sat down. "I'm all ears."

"I don't think Tess is coming back to us, Mom. I think she's gone," Francis said softly, but with conviction.

Mary choked back a sob. "I know. I had a dream. But I didn't want to believe it... Oh, Francis, what are we going to do if it's true?" She hugged him fiercely.

"I don't know, Mom. I don't know," Francis said helplessly, as he put his arms around her.

*****

"Sally, Sally," her mother said gently, shaking her.

Sally had found herself taking a catnap after all the anxiety and worry of the day. She yawned and blinked at her mother's frame. Patricia's red-rimmed eyes didn't surprise her because she had been crying so much lately. However, she was surprised to see her looking graver than usual.

"There's something I need to tell you, Sally. I think I've been afraid to say it, or even think it, but I've known it right from the moment I heard it." There was a brief pause, as Sally looked at her mother expectantly. "I don't think Craig is coming back to us. I think he's gone for good," Patricia said as her voice broke.

"What do you mean, Mom?" Sally asked, bewildered.

"At first, I thought he had abandoned us. But I know Craig. He wouldn't do that to us. The fact that he hasn't got in touch since is either because he's hurt, or worse...." She couldn't go on.

"Oh, Mom, no...not that. Don't say that," Sally said and hugged her mother.

"I don't know what to do, Sally. I honestly don't know," Patricia said hopelessly.

And though they didn't know it then, Craig's and Tess's families were united, at that very moment, in common grief and in death of hope.

*****

Rachel walked in the direction the voice behind her told her to go and gasped in awe at the beauty surrounding her. He told her what to eat and showed her where to sleep. He was constantly talking to her.

Another day passed, but she felt at peace. She was filled with a strange sense of well-being, and all her worries about getting home and seeing Brian slipped away as she listened to all the things the voice told her.

She didn't fully understand them, but she was happy to hear them because the voice was the voice of the one who loved her and who she was learning to love. She felt she could follow Him anywhere.

"Blessed are the pure in heart, for they shall see God... Blessed are you when people persecute you and despitefully use you because of Me, for great is your reward in heaven. Let your light so shine before men that they may see your good deeds and glorify your Father in heaven," the voice whispered softly.

She walked along until she came near a spring that looked quite familiar. She could just hear Brian's teasing voice; "*That's why you love me.*" She really missed him, and she felt a pang of pain as the image of his face came before her. She suddenly felt like going back to meet him. How could she have left him?

"Whoever wants to be My disciple must deny himself, take up his cross, and follow Me," the voice whispered. But she was beginning to think the cross would be too much for her to bear if it meant leaving Brian.

"I love him so much," she told her newfound friend with tears in her eyes.

The voice didn't say anything, and Rachel wondered at the silence. She kept walking along till she came to the foot of a cave. "Where are we going?" she asked the unseen hand that guided her along, but there was no answer.

She walked to the entrance of the cave and saw that there were glowing coals within it. It seemed like there were rows of burning coals through the whole length of the cave. She wondered who could have put them there.

"Come," the voice said, pulling her forward. "Now, it is time for you to die."

*****

Kevin stirred the contents of the glass then downed the vodka and wiped his mouth ruefully. Some of his co-workers had the nerve to begin suggesting to him that they should have a memorial. Put it all behind him. But Kevin refused to consider it; how could he be having a memorial for his son? That wasn't the plan!

With Donna's praying and talking about God, he found himself thinking strange thoughts; thoughts formerly alien to him. He was wondering about the afterlife. Was there even such a thing? And if there was, how had he prepared his son? Not very well, he thought.

He knew so little about it himself. If his son was dead, how was he sure he would see him again? He wished he had found out more about these things before now, and Donna seemed so sure about God and Jesus and heaven that it intimidated him. He had felt he still had years to think about all that. His son too should have had that kind of time to consider religion, but now, it seemed like time had run out for Brian.

He shook his head; he shouldn't think like that. However, at night he often dreamt that he was looking for Brian, and then the dream would merge into him becoming a child, frightened of his father's footsteps and inevitable beating. The sense of dread he felt was harrowing. Even then, he had tried to protect his mother and brother, being the oldest child.

On one occasion, he'd stood up to his father, but that resulted in a trip to the emergency room. His mother had begged him to lie about his bruises. Several times, before she died, he'd tried to convince her to leave him, but she'd just kept assuring him that his dad was not a monster. He always wondered how she couldn't see it.

His brother had moved away to Australia as soon as he could manage it, possibly to escape the demons of his childhood. Kevin had stayed, and he felt he had successfully fought those demons. Until now. Now, he was terrified. He felt like he was a child again; totally helpless.

21

Chapter 21

Rachel gasped in horror as the voice said, "Now, it is time for you to die."

What did that mean? Surely, her Friend would not want to kill her? He loved her!

"Rachel, I want you to walk through this cave," the voice directed.

Rachel's mind revolted. Her footwear was flimsy at best, and this meant literally walking through fire. It was crazy!

"It's impossible," she told her Friend.

"*When you walk through the waters, I will be with you, when you pass through the rivers, it will not sweep over you. When you walk through the fire, you will not be burned, the flames will not set you ablaze*," He replied gently

Rachel stood staring at the entrance of the cave, wondering if she was hallucinating. Perhaps someone had given her LSD or something, and this was a very bad trip. She had gone through many dangers, certainly, but to deliberately walk-through fire was another matter. And to what end?

"Rachel, My beloved, let not your heart be troubled. You

believe in God; believe also in Me," the voice said.

Rachel took a step forward, then a step back. The voice of reason was telling her to leave and try to find her way back to Brian because she had begun hearing things, and her journey through the jungle had fried her brain. Still, His voice persisted.

"When you walk through the fire, you will not be burned…"

Rachel took a deep breath and decided to believe her unseen Friend. He said He would be right beside her. She took a step, then two steps, and then she was on the coals.

A sharp, searing pain shot through her feet, and she screamed. The coals were red-hot! She could smell the odor of burnt flesh. Still, she took another step forward while crying, sweating, and screaming. But, even in her pain, she had the strange sense that someone was screaming with her.

Slowly, but surely, with intense pain coursing through her body, she reached the other end of the cave. And when she emerged into the sunshine, too much in pain to walk any longer, she collapsed and lapsed into unconsciousness.

*****

Donna dropped the receiver with a sigh. She wondered if she should give up too like Craig's mother appeared to be doing.

"He's never left me alone this long," Patricia sobbed. "I think something terrible has happened to him. My Craig is gone!"

Donna tried to pacify her, but the woman wouldn't be consoled.

"No, it's hopeless. I know he's gone. I would have loved to give him a good burial, but I'll settle for a memorial. When are you planning on having yours, Mrs. Anderson?"

Donna told the woman in as gentle a tone as she could muster that she had no plans on doing anything of the sort yet.

"Oh, I guess you'll need some time to get used to it," the well-meaning woman had said, sniffing. "Call me when you're ready."

Donna sat down on the sofa, trying to convince herself that she would never need to be ready. She was failing miserably at the moment.

*****

Rachel awakened to the sun caressing her face and the sounds of birds singing. She had never felt better. She looked down at her feet; the skin underneath was unbroken, whole. The burns had disappeared!

She looked around. The cave too had disappeared. Had it all been a dream?

"You are My daughter, and today, I have become your Father," the voice whispered to her.

Rachel couldn't describe the sensation she felt. She felt alive, renewed, and pure! She felt so glad He had adopted her. She knew He would always be there for her and that she could rely on Him. He would never leave her, for He was nothing like her biological father.

A feeling of warmth descended in her chest. Was this what having a Heavenly Father felt like?

"Thank You, Father. I love You and will follow You forever," she whispered to Him, fully content. She rested her head on the grass, just basking in the glow of His love for her.

"Rachel, go now and tell others what I have done for you," the voice said.

Rachel didn't understand. Tell *others*? But there was no one here in this part of the jungle apart from her. Suddenly, it was clear. That meant she wasn't going to stay in the jungle any longer. She was going home!

She began running in the direction the voice told her to go.

*****

Sierra woke up panting and in a sweat. She had to hold her aching chest for a few seconds. The dream seemed so vivid, so real.

She had been running in a field, but strangely, it seemed she was trying to run in a dozen different directions at once. She didn't seem to know where to go, and she was getting more confused and scared the more she ran.

Then, out of nowhere, she heard Rachel's voice; "This way, Mom! Run this way!"

She didn't know which direction Rachel meant, and as she couldn't see her, she tried frantically to run in the direction of the voice she had heard. But when she began running in one direction, Rachel's voice sprang from another direction, urging her to run the other way, and she began running again but finally collapsed out of sheer exhaustion. Then she woke up.

Sierra crawled out of bed and went to the kitchen to get herself a cup of coffee. The dream was surreal, and she couldn't even begin to think about what it might mean. Perhaps it meant nothing, and it was just because she was always thinking about Rachel, so her subconscious had to reflect that. But it seemed more likely to be something deeper. It seemed as if Rachel was trying to pass across a message to her.

As she sipped her coffee, she knew one thing was sure; whatever happened after all this, she would never be the same again, and she would not treat Rachel the same way again. If she ever got to see Rachel after all this, her rendezvous with an unknown boyfriend wouldn't matter as long as she could hold her daughter in her arms again.

*****

Rachel did not understand where the strength came from. She knew she must have run for hours, but she could feel no fatigue. She could only hear the voice of the Father urging her on.

Gradually, the clear, flat landscape changed, and she had to climb a mountain that was quite high and steep, but to her body, it seemed no more tasking than climbing an anthill. She asked her Father why she seemed so strong and untiring, and He told her, "*Those that wait upon the Lord shall renew their strength, they shall mount up with wings like eagles, they shall walk and not be weary, they shall run and not faint.*"

Rachel found herself grinning from ear to ear. And Brian had thought she couldn't survive in the wild on her own! *Ha!* If only he could see her now.

She wondered again if he was still alive. Her mind refused to accept the possibility that he might be dead like Tess and, probably, Craig. When she got out of this place, she would find a way to rescue him somehow. Brian might be right that she was no good on her own, but with the help of her Heavenly Father, she felt she could do absolutely anything!

She ran on, and then the landscape changed again, and she was in a valley. The weather changed too. It suddenly grew misty and cloudy, and a chill filled the air. She shivered but ran on and began to hear other voices, not her Father's, talking to her.

"I don't like this place," she told her Father. But she couldn't hear His reply. It began getting so foggy, she couldn't see and had to stop running.

She called out to her Father but couldn't hear His answer. Something struck her across the face, and she nearly fell. She became scared and started screaming. But no one answered.

No voice told her anything. Rachel was bewildered. Where had her Father gone?

*****

"They're almost here, Kev," Donna said to her husband. "I can feel it."

They were sitting on the sofa in front of the television, watching the news and drinking hot chocolate. Kevin shrugged. He still didn't know what to make of his wife's strange ramblings. He, for one, had decided that whether Donna liked it or not, there would be a memorial for the four children by the following week.

He was tired of living in limbo. The unknown seemed so scary. It was better that they accept the truth.

Donna turned her face to his. "You've got to believe me, Kevin. They're coming. They'll soon be here." She knew it to be true.

"Fine. I hear you," Kevin said resignedly.

"Do you suppose they'll call to tell us when they arrive?" Donna asked him.

"How the hell am I supposed to know? You're the one who said they are coming," he said belligerently.

"Oh, it doesn't matter if they call or not. They'll soon be here, that's what counts," Donna said, her tone weirdly optimistic.

Kevin gave her an odd look but said nothing. He hoped that Brian's disappearance wasn't proving too much for his wife's mental health. He would not be able to deal with her having a nervous breakdown.

She would have to accept the truth soon. But by God, he

wished with all his heart that her crazy prediction would come true.

*****

Rachel wondered what to do. She couldn't see nor could she hear her Father's voice, and she wasn't even sure she was walking in the right direction anymore. Something she had heard a long time ago came to her mind; "*The Lord is my shepherd; I shall not want... I shall not be afraid, not even if I walk through the valley of the shadow of death, for You are with me...*" She began to say the words aloud and continued walking even though she couldn't see.

Gradually, the mist cleared, the mocking voices ceased, the sun came out, and she could run again.

"Where were You, Father? I was so scared," she told Him.

"I am right beside you, always," He replied.

"But I couldn't hear You," she complained.

"Sometimes, you might not hear Me, but never doubt for one second that I am with You. For when You think I am farthest, that is when I am nearest."

Rachel pondered this as she ran and came to a river. The river was long and wide, but with logs placed at strategic points on the river, she managed to cross it in three strides without even getting wet. She ran on and came to a junction. She asked her Father which way to go, and He told her to run straight on. Rachel continued running until her right foot struck something, and she almost fell.

It was the book! She picked it up like long-lost treasure and held it to her chest. She opened it to see what was inside. It read: "**To him who overcomes, I will grant the crown of life.**"

Rachel closed the book and wondered if she should carry it

but remembered that her Heavenly Father told her that she now had Him, and He was the Book. She dropped it on the ground; maybe someone else might need it.

She continued running and then came out on a highway. There seemed to be no traffic. Perhaps few people traveled this route, she thought.

Her strength suddenly seemed to have given out, and she collapsed on the edge of the road, panting so hard, she thought her lungs would burst. "Alright, Father," she said between breaths. "I seem to have run as far as I can go. I can't run all the way home, can I? Now, what's next?"

22

Chapter 22

J im was tired, and it showed in the worry lines on his grizzled face. The truck was sputtering, and it seemed like it was finally going to give up. The eighteen-wheeler truck has been Jim's companion for eight solid years, and he reckoned it had good reason to be weary after spending so many long hours on the road day after day.

He put on the stereo and listened to his favorite Kenny Rogers tape. He was humming along when he noticed a blur of movement on the road.

Holy Moses! Wasn't that a young lady by the side of the road? What was she doing on Highway I-31?

He pulled over to take a closer look and got out of the truck. She looked like she might be sleeping.

"Hello, lady," he said, placing a hand on her shoulder.

She jumped and glanced at him. Then in the same breath, with her arms upraised, she said, "Thank You, Father!"

Jim looked at her strangely and said, "You seem to be a long way from home, young lady."

Rachel's jaw dropped. "You...you speak English?"

"I think I might accuse you of the same thing," Jim said, raising his eyebrows.

"Oh, just that I wasn't sure where we were all this time. It's a long story…"

Jim chuckled. "Sounds like it. I'd like to hear all about it. For your information, you are currently in God's own country, specifically North Carolina."

"You mean we're in North Carolina?" Rachel asked, incredulous.

"Last sign I checked, that's what it told me," Jim replied, his eyes crinkling.

"Where are you from, kid?"

Rachel got up and shook off the grass from her jeans. "Sir, my name's Rachel, and I'm from New York. Don't ask me how I got here because I really don't know myself, and whatever I tell you, you're not going to believe me."

"Name's Jim," he said, holding out his hand. "Don't be too sure I won't believe your story. I've heard some wild stories in my time." He gestured towards the truck. "Why don't you hop on in, and I'll see how far we can get you."

Rachel nodded gratefully and headed into the truck with Jim supporting her.

"It doesn't have fancy seats, but it'll do," he said confidently. "I've got a couple of sandwiches in the bag. I suppose you're hungry?"

As if in answer, Rachel's stomach rumbled. She felt embarrassed and accepted the sandwiches gratefully. Jim revved up the engine, and the truck was just about to move when a voice shouted in front of them; "Stop! Wait!"

Rachel looked up from her sandwiches to see who was waving them down and nearly collapsed on the front seat.

*****

Donna knew Kevin thought she was crazy. But she could hardly hold the sense of expectation in her heart. Her son was coming home!

She had to admit that she didn't know exactly when that would be, but she knew the hour was near. She wondered if she should have a party for him but felt that Kevin would not buy into the idea. Brian had only been away for a few days, but it felt like months! So, she busied herself with cleaning up Brian's room and arranging his things just so.

She wanted everything to be nice and ready for him when he arrived.

*****

Rachel's legs were shaking, but she managed to swing them out of Jim's truck and rush to the figure in front of her.

"Brian!" she screamed, hugging him fiercely and kissing his cheek.

He grasped her shoulders and pulled her away from him to take a good look at her. "I thought you were dead!" Brian exclaimed.

"So did I!" Rachel confessed.

"This is amazing!"

"It's incredible!"

Jim had come out of the truck and was walking towards them. "Are you kids going to come in the truck and tell me what this is all about?" he demanded.

"In a minute, Sir," Brian replied. He looked hard at Rachel. "So, I guess you've met Him too."

"Who?"

"The Man who saved both our lives..."

Rachel knew exactly who he meant. "Uh-huh," she nodded. "And what an encounter it was.

Brian smiled, and taking her arm, they headed into the truck.

*****

Sierra Menendez had a funny feeling in her chest when she woke up that morning. She didn't know how she knew, but she knew today was going to be the day. She was going to hear news of Rachel that day. She just knew it.

She considered calling Donna to ask her if she had heard anything but decided against it. She knew Mrs. Anderson would notify her as soon as she heard something. No use worrying the woman unnecessarily. Spreading her morning paper on the table, she settled down to wait.

*****

Three hours, two sandwiches, and about forty miles later, Jim had listened to the bare essentials of their incredible tale. He chuckled when they finished.

"You know, your story isn't that wild. In fact, I've heard a couple of stories like yours. I bet many people could tell a tale similar to yours."

"How's that?" Rachel asked, not comprehending.

He pointed to a black leather-bound book that lay near his windshield. "Stories like yours are inside here," he said.

They both peered at the inscription on the front of the book. It was written in gold lettering: 'The Holy Bible.'

Brian and Rachel glanced at each other with a knowing look and a fresh understanding.

The Epilogue

"Hurry up," Sierra said as she put finishing touches to her makeup. "We don't want to be late."

Rachel glanced at her mother's reflection in the mirror and smiled. Her mother was very eager to start her own journey. There was no hurry now, was there? But obviously, her mother wanted to run, not walk.

She remembered the look of joy, disbelief, and relief, all rolled into one, on her mother's face when she had arrived home. Brian and his family had dropped her off and her mother seemed torn between wanting to give Brian a piece of her mind and hugging everyone fiercely. Her mother had talked about grounding her for a year initially but after having a conversation with Brian when he came to visit the next day, she no longer had any concerns about their relationship. She felt he was very respectful and protective of Rachel. She has become so comfortable with their relationship, she asked Brian to pick them up and take them to church.

They hurried through breakfast and piled into the car, with Brian and Rachel in front while her mother sat in the back. Brian put his hand over Rachel's. He was glad and grateful that they were still together after the ordeal, and their faith had brought them even closer together. His parents would be meeting them at the church.

"I hope we get to do this over and over again, for a long, long time," Brian said softly.

Rachel squeezed his hand. She loved going to church with him and just being with him in general. "We will."

They pulled out of the driveway and onto the highway and arrived at the building ten minutes later. As Brian parked, Rachel noticed his parents approaching the curb and waved. Kevin and Donna smiled back as they parked and approached the tall building, which had a simple wooden cross on top of it. After Brian came back home, Kevin felt he could no longer deny the existence of the supernatural. And he was eager to find out everything he could about it.

As if on cue, another car arrived, and Francis, Sally, and their mothers stepped out. It felt like all was complete.

It had been tough accepting the news of Tess's death and Craig's disappearance, and they'd had to do a lot of grieving and soul-searching, but they realized that they too had to begin their own journeys. And they were doing it in the best possible way - together. Sally and Francis were becoming quite close already. One could almost think that they were brother and sister. The two bereaved mothers also found comfort in each other.

Brian held the door open for Mrs. Menendez as she stepped out of the car, her face suffused with pleasure. It didn't have stained glass windows like the Catholic church she went to for her monthly confession, and the architecture was simple, but Sierra didn't care. Without another word to them, she stepped into the building.

Brian grinned at Rachel. "She just can't wait to meet Him, can she?"

Rachel nodded. People were at different stages in the journey. Take Donna for instance. She had stalled for a while on the trip but was continuing her journey. People like Tess and Craig never wanted to start the journey at all. Rachel sometimes felt a twinge of guilt that she had survived, and others hadn't, and Brian admitted to having this feeling as well, but they were both beyond grateful that they had been given another chance.

To everyone who had seen both Rachel and Brian on their return home, it seemed like their adventure had finally ended, but Rachel and Brian both knew that wasn't true. They knew the journey hadn't ended; it wasn't even close to the end.

Brian took Rachel's arm. "Shall we?" he asked, bowing to her.

She smiled and nodded, and together, they walked into the building, ready to start the journey. For their real journey, in truth, had only just begun.

THE END.

Author's Note

This is a work of fiction, but the truth of the matter is that all of us are on that journey, whether we like it or not. All too soon, the journey will come to an end. The way we go about our journey determines whether we live or die. And you can't rightly go on a journey without a proper map. That was why Brian and Rachel had a guidebook.

It won't do to try to go on your own like Craig and Tess. You'll only get lost. So, what can we do? We can follow the example of Brian and Rachel.

1. **Acknowledge that you are not perfect.** That's what Rachel, Brian, and Craig discovered at the river. "*For all have sinned and come short of the glory of God*" (Rom 3:23).

2. **Turn away from your sins.** It's not enough just to say that you're not perfect. Rachel kept warning Brian and herself to keep from doing some of the things they had done before. "*Therefore, I loathe and abhor myself and repent in sackcloth and ashes*" (Job 42:6).

3. **Surrender.** Don't struggle against sin because you can't win. Leave your burdens and your sins at the feet of Jesus. Rachel and Brian surrendered when they stopped struggling in the swamp. "*For being ignorant of the righteousness that God ascribes and seeking to establish a righteousness of their own, they did not obey or submit themselves to God's*

righteousness" (Rom 10:3).

4. **Ask for mercy.** Rachel pleaded for God's mercy when they were in the pit. "*Let Your face shine on Your servant; save me for Your mercy's sake and in Your loving kindness*" (Psalms 31:16).

5. **Believe.** Don't scoff because it seems too simple. Believe that you have been saved because you have. Rachel and Brian both came to believe in the One who had saved their lives. Why shouldn't you? "*Do not let your hearts be troubled...believe in God, believe also in Me*" (John 14:1).

Wishing you a fulfilling journey,

Victoria Olasegha.

About the Author

Victoria Olasegha is a psychiatrist who is passionate about weaving stories that help others enrich their relationships but also draws them into a closer relationship with God. She is a passionate mental health advocate, and this reflects in her writing. She draws on her own experiences and the experiences of others to create rich, empowering, and relatable stories. When she is not working with people, writing, or thinking of what next to write, she makes her home in Manchester with her family, where she is a wife and mother.

You can connect with me on:
- https://linktr.ee/vickysegha
- https://facebook.com/victoriaolasegha
- https://instagram.com/vickysegha

Also by Victoria Olasegha

Bedazzled

A promise...

Suddenly shattered...

A mystery to unravel...

Tade: A man intent on dazzling his wife but keeping a lot of secrets...

Foluke: Revels in her husband's love but circumstances plunge her into a life threatening enigma...

Tunde: A chance meeting.a forging of hearts Would he be the answer to the

dilemma?

Overcoming the Odds

The realities of our time reveal a yawning difference between the older and younger generations. Research has shown that it is often very challenging to attempt to repair the fractured relationships between parents and their teenagers. This book aims to show that there are ways in which this could be overcome. Using prose, it gives stimulating accounts of this possibility and encourages readers of both generations to take a honest look at themselves and reflect, and suggests that they can create new and ingenious ways of improving their family relationships

Printed in Great Britain
by Amazon

41666351R00098